Escape the Dollhouse

WILLIAM PHILLIPS

First Edition April 2025

ISBN: 979-8-218-64830-5

Printed in the United States of America

Cover Art by Keith Goulette

For Max

You were my constant companion, quietly present through every word I wrote. I'm grateful the pandemic gave us that unexpected, precious year—your last, and our closest.

PART I

1

June 17th, 2019

The first rays of the sun peeked over the horizon. There was nothing but sand and haze covering the entire landscape. This was the only time in the desert where the temperature was bearable. The cold, dry nights hid any signs of life. The sizzling, dehydrated days were worse. In the harsh daylight, it was easy to see that the night wasn't hiding anything. There were no signs of life. Just a dirt road and even landscape.

That made working in the desert even worse. Even though they had only been there for a few days, Chris could never get used to the heat. He would seek shade as much as he could, but there was little to be found.

Today, he found himself standing in the rising sun in the middle of the desert. If he looked to the left, he could see the dirt road that brought him here. To his right, there was a slight hint of a mountain on the horizon. Near the mountain, he could see a power turbine spinning in the distance.

He lifted his hand to shield his eyes as the sun continued to rise. The heat continued to rise as well. Chris guessed it had to be close to 90 degrees already. He was sure today would hit 115 like the last few days have. He moved his hand from shielding his eyes and used the back of it and his forearm to wipe a thick spray of sweat from his forehead.

Chris squinted as some of the sweat ran down into his eyes. He blinked a few times to get it out and as his eyes began to focus again, he noticed a figure approach him. He blinked a few more times to clear the stinging sweat from his eyes. As his vision began to return to normal, he recognized the figure as Frank.

"Hey man," Frank said as he approached.

"Hey," Chris said.

"You look like you could use one of these," Frank said. He put the small, dirty cooler that he was carrying down on the ground. He bent over, slid it open, and pulled out two bottles of water, dripping in perspiration.

"You read my mind," Chris replied.

They turned in unison as Frank pointed at a large rock formation a few yards behind Chris. They walked back to it and perched themselves on the side.

Chris twisted off the cap on the bottle of water and lifted it to his lips. The water felt cool and refreshing on his dry, chapped lips. He drank until the bottle was half empty and stopped. It hurt momentarily. Too much cold going into someone who was overheating. He quickly got over the pain, and a refreshing feeling fell over him. He took another smaller drink as Frank began talking.

"Looks like we're the first ones here." He paused. "Again."

"Sounds about right. I'd rather get the workday over with before the heat gets unbearable again. But I guess it's too much to ask everyone to get up early. I hate working out here. Why can't we go back to building condos in the city?"

"I thought you were afraid of heights?" Frank ribbed.

"I am. But I'd rather be 10 stories up than in 115-degree heat. Besides, when we're in the city, we get started on time, and we're out of there early."

"True," Frank said. "But you know Young or the rest of the crew can't get their act together to get here…" He trailed off. Before Frank could finish his thought, something caught his eye in the distance.

Chris looked over at him to see why he stopped talking and noticed Frank staring at something off in the distance. Chris followed his gaze to see what he was looking at. There was a car, probably a mile off in the distance, speeding down the dirt road. Chris immediately thought that they would never have seen it from that far away if they hadn't been in the flat, horizontal desert.

The car was leaving a plume of dust in its wake. It looked almost as if a dust storm was barreling straight toward them.

"Probably Young trying to get here on time." Chris chuckled, taking another swig of his water.

"I don't think so," Frank said. "The rest of the crew all drive trucks." He squinted to see better. "That looks like a black car. A town car or a limo or something."

Chris squinted to get a better view as the car continued to barrel toward them. Frank was right. It was some sort of a town car or something.

As the car bounced down the dirt road toward them, Chris began to feel uneasy.

"Why would a limo be all the way out here at the crack of dawn?" He asked.

Frank shrugged. "Something doesn't seem quite right about this."

Chris pushed himself off the rock and used his hand again to shield the light. He wanted a better look. In the distance, he could see that the car was slowing down, and the cloud of dust trailing behind it was getting smaller.

"I think they're stopping," Chris said.

Frank stood next to him as they watched the car come to a stop about half a mile away.

The car stopped, and immediately, the trunk popped open. Chris and Frank watched as a tall, thin man in a suit hopped out of the driver's side and ran back toward the trunk. A shorter, rounder man followed out of the passenger's side and met the tall man at the trunk. They pulled 2 shovels out of the trunk and ran to the driver's side of the car. They began to dig furiously.

"What the hell are they digging?" Frank asked.

"I don't know. This is really weird."

The digging continued until they had what Chris guessed was a fairly large size hole. The desert sand may have been soft on top, but there was a layer of hard rock just below it, so digging a hole that size wouldn't have been easy.

The two men staggered back to the trunk of the car. It was obvious, even from half a mile away, that the combination of physical exertion and the desert heat was getting to them. They disappeared behind the open trunk, and the shorter, rounder man reappeared with a black box. From Chris's perspective, it was maybe double the size of a large shoe box.

The man dropped the box into the hole. He looked around. Chris could see him screaming something back to the car, but he was too far away to hear. He could only hear the silence of the desert around him.

The tall, thin man appeared again from behind the open trunk. He yelled something back to the round man and approached him with the two shovels in hand.

Chris and Frank watched again as the men filled in the hole they had just spent so much energy digging.

"Whatever they're burying, they want to make sure no one ever finds it," Frank said.

Chris nodded but couldn't take his eyes off the men.

Within a few minutes, they finished filling back in the hole. The tall man threw the shovels back in the trunk as the round man disappeared back into the passenger's side of the car. The tall man closed the trunk and ran back around to the driver's seat. Within seconds of getting in, the car was in motion again. It did a quick U-turn, blowing up a storm of dust.

Chris had trouble seeing what happened next. Once the dust had settled, he saw only a brief glimpse of the car heading back out of the desert toward town.

"What the hell was that? What do you think they just buried there?" Chris asked.

"There's only one way to find out." Frank smirked.

"No," Chris said hesitantly. "Who knows what it could be. We should just stay out of it. I don't want to get dragged into something that—"

Frank cut him off. "We're going."

Frank started walking toward his beat-up white pickup truck. Chris followed him with some hesitation. He was nervous but curious about what they might find.

Frank jumped into the driver's side of the car. Chris followed slowly and got into the passenger's side. Frank quickly started the car, threw it into gear, and drove toward the freshly filled hole in the desert.

Before Chris could even say anything, Frank pulled up beside the hole. He pushed the gear shifter into the park and hopped out of the truck. Chris joined him and they both met at the side of the filled-in hole.

Chris was right. It was a pretty good size. It was at least three feet by three feet. There was no telling how deep it was.

"Let's dig this up and find out what was so important," Frank exclaimed. He looked like a child on Christmas about to unwrap a present.

"I'm already sweating like crazy; it's going to be so much work to—" Frank cut him off by bumping into him. He gave him a friendly push out of the way as he made his way to the back of the pickup truck.

Frank clanked around in the bed of the truck. Chris couldn't only partially see what he was doing, but he knew he was looking for something.

Frank reappeared from behind the truck. He had a shovel in one hand and a crowbar in the other.

"I think there's only one shovel back here. You want it, or do you want to see what you can get up with the crowbar?" He asked.

"I'll use the shovel; it's fine," Chris said, defeated. He was in this now, so he might as well help out and dig.

Frank tossed the shovel, and Chris caught it at the top of the handle. Frank hopped around to the other side of the hole and began to loosen and move dirt with the crowbar. Since it was fresh and loose, it was easy to move.

Chris started to dig. As he pushed the shovel into the ground, he was surprised at how easily the earth moved. It was almost like pushing around sand at the beach.

As the hole began to get bigger and bigger, Chris began to grow more apprehensive about what they were going to find. What if it was a buried treasure? The hole was too small to fit a body. What if it was drugs, and the cartel was going to come back and look for it? His mind raced with ideas but came to a screeching halt when his shovel hit the box.

He looked up at Frank. Frank smiled and threw the crowbar aside. He got down on his knees and began to push the sand and rocks aside. Within seconds, he had uncovered the lid of the box.

Chris set the shovel next to him and got down on his hands and knees. The box was about the size he thought of. It wasn't completely square, but it was probably about 24 inches by 18 inches.

It was a hard metal box. The shovel had hit it, and sand and rocks had been dragged across it as they tried to uncover it, leaving scratches all over the top.

"Open it," Frank exclaimed.

Chris reached down and noticed for the first time that his hand was shaking. He took a deep breath, swallowed, and tried to steady his hand. He looked up again at Frank as he gripped the lid of the box.

He wrapped his fingers around the lip of the lid and pulled. It gave way and opened like a book. Chris pushed some of the dirt out of the way so that he could get the lid fully open. When the lid was fully open, he got a clear glimpse of what was inside the box.

He unknowingly held his breath and looked up at Frank. They were both struggling to comprehend what they were seeing. Chris looked back down, unconsciously hoping that what he had seen the first time was a mistake. But it wasn't. There was a baby inside of the box.

The baby was wrapped in a dirty blue blanket, and everything inside the box was covered in dirt. When the fresh air hit the opening lid, the baby took a deep breath and began to cry. It was alive.

"It's a child," Chris was shocked to hear himself say.

"STOP!" A voice screamed. "No, no, no. This is all wrong." Light filled a dark room. The desert scene was being projected onto a screen in a small theater.

"This isn't the take that I asked for," the voice shouted into the air. "He's supposed to say, 'It's a baby.' Can we make a note of that so Mark can edit in the right take?"

The voice belonged to the film's director, Jake Doll.

Jake sat in the front row of the small screening room amongst a small group of faceless people. Mark, the film's editor, sat in the row behind Jake with a group of assistant editors. They furiously took notes as Jake spoke.

"I'm sorry, Jake. I had the wrong take in there," Mark said, sounding hopeless.

Jake stood up in front of the screen and faced the group. "Don't worry about it, we'll get it." The crowd wasn't sure if he was sincere, but he was one of the more likable directors they'd worked with.

"We've been pushing ourselves really hard to get this thing edited in time, and we must have missed that one. I know you mentioned it during our last rough-cut screening." Mark lowered his head.

"These things happen," Jake said. "I know we're all under a lot of stress to get this thing cut and out. This is the first feature, and I just want it to be perfect."

"It will be," a voice radiated from the back of the room. All heads turned to see a magnetic man walking through the door. Immediately, the air in the room became different. Everyone sat up a little bit straighter. Mark went from looking defeated to confident.

Jake exhaled and then took a large gulp of air, which fueled his smile.

"Mr. Rossi, how are you doing this afternoon, sir?" Jake smiled as Mr. Rossi approached him.

He shook Jake's hand and looked him right in the eye. Jake was dwarfed by the man. Jake wasn't short by any conventional calculations, standing nearly six feet tall. Something about Mr. Rossi's presence made him seem even larger than his six-foot-two frame. He also outweighed Jake by 100 pounds.

Jake was skinny and scrawny. He had a habit of wearing clothes that were a size too big, which made his frame underneath them look that much smaller. His blonde hair and glossy blue eyes made him look like a California surfer.

"I'm doing well, Jake. How's the editing going?" Mr. Rossi asked.

"It's going really well. We have a solid rough cut and are making a few more tweaks, and it will be ready for…" He trailed off. In all honesty, this was Jake's first film, and he wasn't quite sure what was next.

"Look, you have Mark here. He'd edited hundreds of these things. Just listen to him."

Jake glanced over at Mark. He was avoiding eye contact.

"You choose the takes and let Mark make them flow," Mr. Rossi finished his thought.

"Yes, sir," was the only thing that Jake could manage.

"I expect you to have this thing locked and completed ASAP. We have a release date looming, and I can't move it. This thing won't make any money if we have to delay it into the holiday season."

"Yes, sir." Jake again couldn't do anything but agree.

"Great," Mr. Rossi exclaimed. "Now, choose your takes and let Mark work his magic."

He exited the room as quickly as he came, and you could feel him suck all of the tension out of the room when he left. The small group of people made eye contact with each other again and started to take deep breaths.

Jake looked Mark in the eye. "Okay, let's try this again."

2

June 17th, 1990

      Stephen pushed another tape into the VCR and sat back down on a shabby-looking couch.

      He sat in an apartment in West Hollywood. It was an unusually cool summer day, but he had all the windows open anyway. There was some noise coming in from the street outside, but it didn't bother Stephen.

      It was one of the rare cases when he had the apartment to himself. His roommate had booked an out-of-town gig, and he had three full days to himself.

      Stephen had long, shaggy, sandy blonde hair. His blue eyes were nearly hidden behind his hair, which nearly touched his nose. He wore no shirt and a pair of neon pink shorts. He was in his mid-twenties and was still in that stage of life where he could eat anything and still keep his physique. He would go to the gym once or twice a week but never put much stock into it.

The TV flashed to life. Stephen looked up as static filled the screen and then down again at the piles of videotapes all over the floor. Each had a sticker on the spine that said "Video Dating Experts" and a woman's name. There was a Vicky, a Diana, a Kelly, a Natasha, and the one that Stephen had just put into the VCR said Melanie.

Within moments, Melanie appeared on the screen. She was the complete opposite of Stephen. She had short, pitch-black hair and sharp features. Stephen could blend in with a crowd of Southern Californian men, but Melanie would stand out.

She faced the camera, which gave the effect that she was speaking directly to Stephen. "Hi, I'm Melanie." Her cadence was distinct, reminiscent of a valley girl, and it caught Stephen off-guard.

"I am like very independent. I like going to the mall and can like spend so much money at one." She giggled.

Stephen rolled his eyes. He picked up the remote control and hit a button, and Melanie was gone as quickly as she appeared. He let out an exhale and dropped the remote back on the couch.

He mustered the strength to lift himself off the couch and walk across the room to the TV. The VCR was just underneath it. He crouched down, hit the eject button, and with the turn of a gear, the videotape came popping out.

He pulled it the rest of the way out of the machine and tossed the video cassette into a pile of others. He grabbed one at random off of the floor and pushed it into the VCR. He didn't even bother to read the name off of the tape.

Stephen lumbered back over to the couch, collapsing on it. Static again filled the screen. Stephen didn't even have a chance to blink before another woman quickly appeared on the screen.

She was much different than Melanie. She had long, straight blonde hair. Her eyes were either blue or green, but Stephen couldn't tell exactly from the fuzzy videotape. She also looked directly into the camera, but Stephen felt differently this time. It felt like she was looking directly at him. In complete contrast to all the other videos, he watched where the women were looking into a camera. Stephen could feel that this woman was looking at him.

She spoke: "Hi. I've rehearsed this a few times, but I don't want it to feel too scripted, so I'm going to throw out the script and just tell you a little bit about myself."

Wow. Stephen was surprised. She seemed refreshingly honest and straightforward. Without even realizing it, he straightened up on the couch and leaned toward the TV to better see and hear this mystery woman.

"This is my first time trying a dating service like this. My roommate actually talked me into it. I've only been out here in LA for a few months and haven't really met many people."

Stephen understood. He lived in LA all of his life, but he still didn't know that many people.

"I'm 23 years old," she said. "I moved to LA from a small town in Illinois. I am quite driven, and I knew I couldn't spend one more winter in Illinois, so I took a chance and came out here. I've been working as a waitress, but I would love to go back to school and get a degree."

Stephen didn't realize that the more this mystery woman spoke, the larger his smile became.

"I'd like to meet a nice guy somewhere around my age..."

Stephen was 24. He figured that would qualify.

"Someone who has a good head on his shoulders."

Stephen pushed his hair back out of his eyes.

"Someone who has drive and ambition to match mine."

Stephen looked around the small one-bedroom apartment he shared with his roommate, but he didn't let it stop the growing smile on his face.

The mystery woman stopped speaking. You could vaguely hear someone off-camera ask a question. The mystery woman broke eye contact with Stephen to look at someone to the left of the camera.

"Oh." She giggled and turned back to look at Stephen. "I guess that would be helpful."

Stephen wondered what was asked.

"My name is Katie."

Stephen's grin now stretched from ear to ear.

"Hello, Katie."

***

16

The date was set a week later. This was Stephen's first time meeting someone from the video dating service, and the process took a lot longer than he was expecting. He called them the same day he saw Katie's video to let them know he'd like to meet her. But then, they had to send Katie a copy of Stephen's tape to make sure she was interested in meeting him.

Luckily, she was, and they arranged to meet on Friday night at a restaurant near Katie's apartment. Stephen drove in rush hour traffic and left himself extra time just to make sure he wasn't late. He wasn't going to let LA traffic stand in the way of a date with the most beautiful woman he's seen in years.

Stephen thought about that as he drove. She was the most beautiful woman he'd ever seen, even though he had never seen her.

Stephen pulled up in front of the restaurant. It was a typically modern-looking building with plenty of windows. Stephen could see the happy diners inside. He left his car with the valet and stepped inside the restaurant.

It was very busy, with nearly every seat taken. He was happy he remembered to make a reservation. He smiled slightly since he was never that organized to think ahead.

Directly in front of him was a desk with a pretty Los Angeles woman standing in front of him. Stephen took a minute to consider why she was working there. Likely trying to make it as an actress, he thought.

The hostess noticed him looking at her and gave a big, charming smile. "Welcome. Do you have a reservation?" she asked.

Stephen took a step toward her so that they could hear each other better over the music and crowd inside the reservation.

"Yes," he said proudly. "For Stephen. 2 people at 7 PM."

The hostess looked down into a large book with organized handwriting in neat columns. She traced her finger down one of the columns. Stephen looked away and glanced around the waiting room to make sure that Katie hadn't arrived before him. He looked down at his watch. It was 6:42. There's no way she beat him there.

Only three or four other people were standing there waiting. Stephen surveyed them, but none of them were Katie. He didn't realize that he had let out a small sigh of relief.

"I'm sorry, sir," he heard the hostess say. It brought him back to reality. "I don't see any reservation under the name of Stephen.

Stephen looked down for a moment to gather his thoughts, then back up at the hostess. "I'm sorry. There must be some mistake. I called on Monday afternoon and made this reservation. The girl I spoke to on the phone said it was confirmed." His face grew flush with terror. "Can you check again?"

The hostess looked concerned but again ran her finger down one of the columns in the large leather book.

"There's nothing here, I'm terribly sorry," she said again.

"Look," Stephen said with a sincerity in his voice. "I'm meeting someone here for a first date. She's going to be here any minute. I'm sure I called and made a reservation on Monday. Isn't there something you can do to help me out?"

The hostess glanced away from Stephen before delivering the message, "There's currently a two-hour wait for a table, sir."

Stephen's face began to get redder. This time, he wasn't flush with terror but red with anger. He raised his voice a little but maintained his composure. "I can't wait two hours. I need to have a table in..." he trailed off. He looked down at his watch. 6:44 PM. "16 minutes."

"Let me see if there's anything I can do," the hostess said. Then, she abandoned her post and disappeared into the restaurant's sea of patrons.

Stephen exhaled and swiftly turned to face the door. He saw a familiar face standing in front of him. It was Katie. She looked exactly as she did in her video but was somehow different in person. She almost seemed to glow and radiate an energy that Stephen could feel.

"Hi," she said, noticing him. She lifted her hand for a little wave.

"Hi," he said. He couldn't think of anything else to say.

"I'm Katie," she said. He stood there, silent for a moment, his face draining from bright red to white in a matter of seconds.

"I'm Stephen," he said, stumbling over his words. He held out his hand to shake hers just as she went in for a hug. They met in the middle with an awkward exchange, with Stephen's hand pressed against her torso, her pulling on his shoulders.

They both awkwardly laughed it off and pulled out of their odd embrace.

"It's so nice to finally meet you," Katie said, brushing her long blond hair back.

"You too," he said. They stood in silence for a moment. He wasn't quite sure what to say next. He wasn't sure if he was overwhelmed, but his mind stumbled, and he couldn't get any words to come out.

"Have you been here long?" Katie asked him.

"No," he said, finding a few words. "Only about 5 minutes."

"This is a great place. Have you been here before?"

"No," he replied again. "In fact, I've never really even been over in this part of LA before."

"You've never been to Brentwood?" She was curious.

Before he could answer, the hostess appeared again out of the sea of diners. She approached Stephen, who was fixated on Katie and didn't notice her arrival.

"I'm terribly sorry sir, but we'll try to fit you in, but it's still going to be about an hour."

Stephen looked over at her and began to turn red again. Katie noticed and jumped right in.

"Emily?" she asked.

The hostess met her gaze, and a huge smile grew on her face. "Katie!" Emily exclaimed.

"Oh my god," Katie exclaimed. They embraced quickly, nearly pushing Stephen out of the way.

After releasing Emily from the hug, Katie again pushed her hair back into place. Stephen noticed for the first time how perfect her nails were. They were a soft pink color and perfectly shaped. He'd never noticed that kind of detail on anyone before.

'I didn't know you worked here," Katie said to Emily.

"Yes, just part-time to pay the bills while I was auditioning."

Stephen was right. She was an actress.

"This is Stephen," Katie said, turning slightly in his direction. His face was still red, but he was silent.

"We've met," Emily said.

"Emily was one of the first people I met in LA. We took a Tae Bo class together."

"Nice to meet you, Emily," Stephen managed to blurt out.

"Is there a problem with our reservation?" Katie asked, with a smile and charm that nearly caught Stephen off guard.

"No," Emily said. She looked over at Stephen. "I'll get you two in. Don't worry about it. It will just be a few minutes."

"Oh, Em. Thank you so much," Katie said, showing off her charm again.

Within a few minutes, they were seated at a table across from each other, getting to know each other.

3

October 8th, 1990

"Are you almost ready?" Katie yelled from the bathroom.

"Yes," Stephen shouted back from the bedroom.

Katie was putting the final touches on her makeup. The entire bathroom counter was covered in products. Hair care, makeup, and skin creams — she had it all — and she used it all. Stephen had given up on ever seeing the bathroom sink again.

She stood looking in the mirror. Every piece of platinum blonde hair was in place. Her makeup covered her face, but it was subtle. She didn't look like she was made up; she just looked effortlessly perfect.

Stephen appeared in the doorway. She looked him up and down once. She nodded.

They left Katie's apartment and drove to Beverly Hills. Katie drove in her bright red Audi 90 Quattro convertible, but they kept the top up to preserve Katie's hair. She pulled off of Santa Monica Blvd. and headed into The Flats. As they passed mansion after mansion, Stephen looked out of the window. He wanted to live here someday.

Katie made another quick right turn and they were pulling into the curved driveway of one of the bigger houses they had encountered.

"Is this the place?" Stephen asked, looking up at the large, imposing white house in front of them.

"Yes, this is it," Katie said. "Are you ready?"

"Ready," Stephen said. Katie couldn't tell if he really meant it or not.

They climbed out of the car and met at the front door. Katie pushed her hair back one more time to make sure it was in place. She adjusted the collar on Stephen's button-down shirt and tried to push a single wrinkle off of the form-fitting dress she was wearing. She took one more look at Stephen and pressed the doorbell.

It wasn't long before the door swung open. A put-together, middle-aged woman answered the door. She didn't scream "Beverly Hills Wife," but she could fit the bill in a pinch.

"Welcome," she said. "You must be Stephen and Katie."

"Yes," Katie replied, turning on her charm.

"I'm Marissa. Come on in." She stepped aside and welcomed them into the house.

The first thing that Katie noticed was the grandness of everything inside the house. It looked huge from the outside, but from the inside, everything looked even bigger. There was nothing modest about the house. The floors were marble, as far as Katie could see. There were 2 large columns in front of them that reminded Katie of being in a Greek garden. Fresh flower arrangements were on every table.

"Did you have any problems finding the house?" Marissa asked.

"Oh no," Katie replied.

"Everyone else is in the great room and by the pool. It's just this way." Marissa turned and walked deeper into the house.

Katie and Stephen followed closely. Katie gripped Stephen's arm as she walked. She whispered into his ear, "I want to live here someday."

He smiled at her as Marissa led them into the great room. She wasn't kidding. The room must have been 50 feet by 50 feet. A large chandelier made of crystal was the centerpiece, hanging from the center of the room. There were tables with white linen strategically placed around the room. The room was full of people mingling and eating hors d'oeuvres passed on silver trays.

Katie guessed they were the youngest two in the room.

"Make yourselves at home," Marissa said in their general direction as she stepped away and toward a table.

"Oh My God," Katie said when she was sure Marissa was out of earshot. "Will you look at this place?" She gripped Stephen's arm even harder.

"We so do not fit in around here." He laughed at her.

She lightly tapped his arm. "Yes, we do, and we're going to make the most of this opportunity."

"Ok," he replied.

Katie and Stephen had grown very close between the four months they met, and the moment they found themselves standing in the middle of a Beverly Hills party. They shared most of their free time and stayed mostly at Katie's apartment. She did not like the feel of Stephen's bachelor pad in West Hollywood and certainly didn't care for his unrefined roommate.

Katie enjoyed learning more about Stephen and talking about her hopes for the future with him. She wasn't particularly enamored with any one career path, but she knew she wasn't fond of waitressing.

Stephen grew up in Orange County with what Katie described as a certain amount of privilege never afforded to her. Both of Stephen's parents were doctors, both absent throughout much of Stephen's youth due to their demanding job schedules. This led them to make up for their lack of time with the freedom of money.

Stephen never wanted for anything when he was younger. His parents gave freely every time he asked. He always wore the best clothes, drove an expensive (and brand-new) car, and had his full college tuition paid.

Katie wondered why he was living in a modest two-bedroom apartment in West Hollywood with a roommate and minimal furniture. If Katie were in the same situation, she would have a condo by the beach where all of her friends could join her every weekend. She also wouldn't be working as a waitress.

Katie's background was a little different. She grew up in a small town in Ohio. Her parents were neither poor nor rich, so she had the benefit of growing up in a middle-class family. Her neighborhood was mostly white, and Katie fit in with her blonde hair and blue eyes.

She always had the same things as most of her social group. She always had food on her table but had to work (or beg her parents) for nicer clothes. She was often stuck wearing her sister's discarded items. They weren't exactly hand-me-downs, but during their teenage years, her sister worked a part-time job after school and spent every cent she had on designer clothes. After she wore them a few times, she was over it and was nice enough to let Katie have them. They weren't exactly the same size, so most of the clothes were too big for her, but Katie didn't mind. It was better than the discount outfits her mother would buy for her.

Katie was a popular girl in high school. She dated a little, mostly members of the football team, and she was an average student. She wasn't the "queen bee" of the school, but she fell comfortably in with the cheerleaders and drama crowd.

Even though many girls would have killed for Katie's social status in high school, Katie never really felt comfortable with it. She always wanted to be seen and stand out from the crowd. Wearing her sister's clothes, dating the same guys all of her friends had at one point or another, and her ability to float between social groups left Katie feeling rather anonymous. She didn't realize that her social abilities that went beyond her admittedly above-average looks were a gift.

It was this feeling of missing something and not sticking out that led Katie to college in Los Angeles. She was able to get into the art program at UCLA. She wasn't quite sure what she wanted to do, but she always had an interest in art. She thought maybe someday she'd work in a gallery or become an art broker. She didn't really have an artistic side, but she was able to appreciate that in others.

This was one of the things that drew her to Stephen. Although he had been spoiled most of his life, Stephen was able to do well enough in school. His parents pulled some strings and got him into USC, where he studied film.

He was only a few years out of college now and hadn't really done anything to progress his career. But Katie and Stephen had many late-night conversations in bed, during which Stephen confessed to her that the only career path he had ever been interested in pursuing was film directing.

It took her a little while to get this information out of him. Stephen loved to talk. It actually took Katie off guard at first. The first day they met at the restaurant, he seemed a little quiet and reserved. But, on their second date, the floodgates opened, and Stephen talked. Actually, Stephen talked a lot about himself. To the point where Katie felt she had known everything there was to know about him within the first few weeks.

That's why it also caught her off guard when he confessed his chosen career path to her nearly two months into their relationship. It was at that point that Katie realized that even though Stephen loved to talk about himself, she didn't really know as much detailed information about him as she thought.

She had heard all about his high school friends, where he would surf in college, and his favorite foods, but she hadn't really heard much about his relationship with his parents. She didn't know much about why he didn't have any siblings. She certainly had never heard much about his hopes and dreams for the future.

Katie didn't let this stop her, though. She took it on as a challenge. Katie always worked best when she had a challenge in front of her. Something she could focus her drive on. That's part of the reason she ended up in Los Angeles. She could have applied to local schools in Ohio like all of her friends.

Already in her senior year of high school, Katie was starting to feel bored with her life. She didn't want the same things that all of her friends wanted. They just wanted to party, meet guys, and talk about getting married someday.

Sure, Katie could party with the best of them, but she knew from a young age that she didn't want some average mid-western life. She wanted to do something big. She didn't know what that was, but she felt something deep down inside of her, driving her to do something different.

She only applied to UCLA, which was her only choice. She had many arguments with her parents over picking a local school, but Katie had always wanted to live somewhere sunny and warm. She hated the cold, and the winters in Ohio were brutal for her.

After she decided she wanted somewhere warm, that was only left in her mind: Florida or California. She grew up watching the glitz and glam of southern California through TV shows, so that made the choice pretty simple.

After graduating with her bachelor's degree in art, she found it difficult to find a job. She ended up waitressing. She was starting to feel restless and bored again, which is why she signed up for the video dating service. She wasn't necessarily looking for the love of her life, but she was looking for a shock out of the rut she found herself in.

Stephen had definitely done that. The night he confessed he'd like to be a film director someday, Katie had a new mission to focus on: She was going to help Stephen get his first big break.

This is how they ended up at the party. Katie started calling everyone she knew from her UCLA days. She wasn't directly involved in the film program, but many of her friends were. She was looking for some kind of introduction to a producer. In Katie's mind, anyone would do. She could help Stephen, and they could either connect with him or leverage him for another connection.

But it wasn't as easy as she had hoped. She worked her charm over the phone to anyone who would take her call. She chatted with her former classmates about the good-ol'-days but no one was able to make any sort of a meaningful connection for her. She found that most people from the film program were struggling to make it themselves and weren't willing to sacrifice their introductions for her.

Within a week or two, she was growing frustrated with the process. The phone calls had dried up, and she found herself consumed with thinking about what else to do. She was venting to one of her coworkers one day when an idea popped into her head. The restaurant she worked at was located in Brentwood. She wasn't sure how many film people lived in the area, but she was going to give it a shot.

She worked her charm on every table for the following weeks. She smiled and asked questions to try to get to know everyone who looked like they might be a connection. She met a few production assistants, an aspiring writer, and even a few set designers. None of them were able to offer a connection that she thought might help.

Her break finally came about a month after she started trying. A man, she guessed to be in his early forties, was sitting in her section. He carried a rolled-up Variety magazine under his arm. He was slightly overweight, but nothing a little exercise couldn't fix. Katie took his order, made sure she was extra friendly, and thought of an angle while she filled the Diet Coke he ordered.

When she got back to the table with the Diet Coke, he was reading the Variety magazine. Katie used that as an angle and started a conversation with him about the entertainment business. She was able to get out of him that he was a producer. When she asked what he'd worked on, it was actually a few movies that Katie had actually heard of.

She knew that this was her chance. She put on the charm the best she could and flat-out asked him if he would help her. She was fully expecting a rejection, but to her surprise, he accepted.

She and Stephen were now standing in the great room of his house, mingling with his friends and colleagues. She was so proud of herself for making this happen.

"I'll let you know when I see him," Katie said to Stephen. They continued their walk around the great room.

"Do you know who some of these people are?" Stephen asked. He looked around the room and pointed a few people out to Katie. "That's Kevin Meecham. He directed Hard to Live. I loved that movie."

He looked around again and pointed someone else to Katie. "That's Chris James. He has produced like every box office hit in the last ten years."

Katie smiled. She liked seeing Stephen this excited.

Stephen was still looking around to see who else he could spot when Katie grabbed his arm.

"There he is," Katie said, pointing at a man across the room. "Let's go over there."

Katie took a look at Stephen. She had helped him look the part for today. She took his long, surfer-esque hair and slicked it back. She made him trade in his shorts and flip-flops for a collared button-down shirt and loafers.

Katie thought no one would confuse him for an international spy, but it was an improvement.

Katie pushed his hair behind his ear to make sure every strand was in place, and they approached the producer.

Katie caught his eye and let out an over-the-top "hello."

He smiled back at Katie. He was several inches shorter than Stephen and several inches rounder in the waist. His hair, though still there, was starting to thin on top. Stephen watched as he took Katie in his arms and gave her a big embrace. Stephen's face started to turn red as Katie graciously pulled herself free.

"Thank you so much for having us, Gio. I really appreciate it."

Gio made constant eye contact with her.

Katie continued smiling and turned slightly to face Stephen.

"This is who I was telling you about." She turned her arms out in Stephen's direction. "This is Stephen."

Gio finally unlocked his eyes from Katie and extended a hand to Stephen. Stephen grabbed it and shook it with a firm up-and-down motion.

"Pleased to meet you, Stephen," Gio said.

"It's a pleasure to meet you, too."

"I hear you want to direct."

"Yes," Stephen said with a confidence that Katie hadn't heard before.

"Do you have a pitch for me?" Gio asked.

"Yes, sir," Stephen said. He wasn't sure if it was too formal to call him sir, but it was too late to take it back. "I've got a great pitch for you."

"Katie here has been saying nothing but great things about you." Gio chuckled. His gaze focused back on Katie.

"They're all true," Stephen said. "My film starts with—"

Gio cut him off.

"Wait a minute. Wait a minute. I can see you're anxious here, aren't you."

Stephen blushed a little.

"Did Marissa meet you at the door?" Gio asked.

"Yes, she did," Stephen answered.

"Great, so you've met her then. She's my assistant."

Katie chuckled. "I assumed she was your wife."

It was Gio's turn to chuckle. "My wife is probably over somewhere at the bar."

Katie and Stephen returned the laugh in nearly the exact same tone. The joke wasn't funny, but they were both trying their hardest to pretend it was.

"Look," Gio said, pointing to the other side of the room. "Marissa is right over there."

Katie and Stephen both turned their heads to see Marissa chatting with someone on the other side of the room.

"Stephen," Gio continued. "Why don't you go over there and let Marissa know that first thing Monday, you want to come into the office. I'll be happy to hear your pitch then. If it's half as good as Katie here says it is, I'm sure I'll love it."

"Yes, that would be great," Stephen said.

"Go on. Go over there and grab her now before she runs away and we lose track of her."

Gio fixed his gaze back on Katie.

Katie smiled at Stephen.

"Yes, sir. Thank you very much. I really appreciate it."

Stephen headed in the direction of Marissa, leaving Gio and Katie together.

"Thank you so much, Gio. This is really so nice of you to do. I realize that you don't know me that well, and it's a really kind thing of you to do to help us out."

"It's no problem, my dear. I wouldn't have gotten my first break without someone helping me out. I'm just passing on the favor. And, for your other point, you're right."

Katie pondered what he meant.

"I don't know you very well. Let's head out to the pool, get you a drink, and you can tell me more about yourself."

Katie smiled. "I'd be happy to do that."

Just as Stephen was approaching Marissa, he glanced over his shoulder toward Katie. He saw Gio put his arm around her lower back and lead her out the door toward the pool. Stephen smiled. This is just what he had dreamed of since he was a boy.

4

June 24th, 1991

Katie could hardly believe it had been a year since she first met Stephen. So much had happened in that past year; she could hardly believe it herself. She flipped open a large suitcase and threw it onto her bed.

Stephen entered the room and looked at the suitcase.

"I guess it's time to start packing," he said, walking past her to the closet. He had been staying exclusively with her at her apartment for the last few months after his lease was up. All of his clothes were shoved in the back of her closet.

The rest of the room was kind of a mess. There was random stuff everywhere. The couple had obviously outgrown her apartment, but she had 2 more months on her lease that she didn't want to break.

"I just keep telling myself you'll only be gone for three months," Katie said, folding a shirt and neatly placing it into the suitcase.

Stephen threw a couple of shirts on the bed and sat down on it next to them. Katie grabbed them and started folding and placing them in the suitcase.

"This is it. I'm going to crush it," Stephen said.

"Yes, you are." Katie chuckled.

Stephen was off to Toronto for three months to film the sequel to "Hard to Live." It took some convincing on Katie's part, but she was able to convince Gio that Stephen would be the perfect person to direct the film.

She was able to overcome all of Gio's objections and even got him to watch the only student short film that Stephen had directed back in college. That was his only experience, but Gio thought it was done well enough that he was confident to give Stephen one of the most coveted jobs in town.

Gio called just a week before and offered Stephen the job and a huge salary but told him he needed to be in Toronto as soon as possible for pre-production.

They spent the week doing everything they could to prepare, including buying warmer clothes. Stephen was convinced that spending three months during the summer in Canada might give him frostbite, as this was his first time in Toronto.

They also had to spend hours at a time on paperwork. Stephen needed to apply for a visa to work in Canada. The studio was able to guide them, but it still required them to do much of the paperwork.

Stephen had little to no patience for that kind of work. He relied almost exclusively on Katie for help.

With Stephen's new job came his new salary. The day Gio called with the offer, Stephen didn't have an agent to negotiate on his behalf, so he took whatever Gio offered him. Neither Katie nor Stephen had ever even considered a number with so many zeros. Since Stephen was going to be in Canada for months and their lease was expiring while he was there, Katie convinced him that they needed to have a joint bank account.

Stephen was clueless when it came to money. He always had more than he needed growing up, so he never learned to manage it. He would just spend without giving it a second thought. He also didn't bat an eye when Katie asked for a joint bank account. Katie doubted that the two million dollar offer to direct "Hard to Live" even registered with Stephen. He probably thought that's what a grocery store clerk made.

The plan was for Katie to look for a new place for them to live and hire movers while Stephen was gone. Katie was looking forward to it. Not so much the moving part, but she now was going to be able to find a place for them to live with virtually no budget limitations. The world was her oyster. This was freedom like she had never known before and she felt elated through all of the tedious work she had to manage over the last week for Stephen.

Stephen sat on the bed talking about himself, which had become a pattern more and more lately, while Katie continued to pack up his stuff. She really had fallen in love with him over the last year. He really was unlike anyone she had ever met.

He could talk, usually at length, about anything that interested him. Katie figured that was his passion showing up verbally. Although he could talk, he didn't possess the social skills that Katie had. She knew when to speak. She knew when to listen. Stephen had only mastered the talking part.

She hoped that would translate well on a set. Surely, it would be good if a director could speak to their actors and crew. They would need to be able to communicate their expectations, and Stephen had mastered saying what he wanted.

It was almost as if he had come into his own over the last year. With Katie's influence, she was able to put him on a path that he had always been lacking in life. His upbringing was so unstructured that when Katie was able to gradually introduce some structure into their lives, Stephen's confidence grew. He had faith in himself. He was able to see his self-worth and speak about the value he brings.

Stephen knew that's why Gio picked him to direct the film. Stephen hadn't directed anything other than his student film before, but he knew that he could do it. He remained confident in front of Gio at all times, and that confidence won him over and got Stephen the job.

"I will take care of everything while you're gone," Katie said.

"Great," Stephen replied.

"I'm going to go out house hunting with Sara tomorrow."

"Great," Stephen replied again.

"I'm not sure where we will look. I was thinking maybe Brentwood or Westwood." She looked over at Stephen and he didn't seem to be paying attention. "Or, maybe Compton. I hear that's nice."

Stephen didn't look up. Katie playfully threw a shirt from the pile at him.

"Hello!" She said. "Are you even listening to me?"

"Oh, yes, you said you're going house hunting."

"Well," she said. "Maybe you were half listening."

"I'm just ready to go," he said.

"You sure know how to make me feel great about myself." She chuckled.

"You know what I mean," he said, almost snapping.

"Of course I do. You've been waiting a long time for an opportunity, and now that it's here, you're ready to jump right in."

"Yes," he said. "I'm so ready."

"Did you pack your passport?" She asked.

"I don't know where it is," he calmly said.

"Don't worry about it. I know it's around here somewhere. I will find it."

The next day, Stephen was on a plane to Toronto, and Katie was in her Audi with her friend Sara. They were on their way to Westwood to look at yet another house for rent. They pulled up in front of a modern-looking house. Katie would tell from the outside that the owners had tried to keep up with it. She saw her realtor, Maggie, waiting for her in the driveway.

Sara and Katie both jumped out of her car and walked over to greet Maggie.

Maggie smirked at them and said, "Absolutely not."

Katie looked up at the house again. It didn't look that bad.

"Why not?" Katie asked.

"For this price, there should be at least two bathrooms and a pool. Inside, there's still shag carpet and a pink bathroom. I won't even let you go in," Maggie said, throwing her hands in the air.

"Ugh," Sara said. "This is the third house today, and they've all been terrible."

Katie looked a little discouraged.

"Look," Maggie said, making direct eye contact with Katie. "I know you said you wanted to stay in Westwood or Brentwood, but are you open to looking a little further outside of the area?"

"How far outside?" Katie asked, almost suspiciously.

"I know that Stephen is in Toronto. And I know with a movie deal like his, he's probably got a big paycheck and a piece of the backend."

Katie didn't even know what "a piece of the backend" meant, but she knew that Stephen did get a very big payday from the gig.

"Okay..." Katie trailed off.

"I found the perfect listing. It's not too far from here. Why don't you let me take you and show you the house that you deserve? I promise it will be worth the drive."

Sara smiled. She was intrigued.

"Fine, fine, fine," Katie said, relenting. "No promises, but let's at least go look."

Sara and Katie hopped back into the car and followed Maggie's Jaguar down Wilshire Blvd. When they hit Santa Monica Blvd., Katie was sure she would take a right and drive them down into Century City or maybe a little further south to Mar Vista. But Maggie led them straight across Wilshire and directly into the heart of Beverly Hills.

She quickly turned off of Wilshire and made their way through several residential neighborhoods.

"What is happening here?" Sara giggled.

Katie tried to pay attention to the road, but her attention was drawn to the ever-growing houses they were passing. They started reasonably enough, but as the houses got bigger, so did the gated driveways.

"There's no way," Katie said to Sara. "She's just torturing us by driving us through Beverly Hills."

Maggie made one final turn and pulled up to a stop in front of the large white house with a red clay roof. As Katie put the car into park, she looked up at the house and was shocked by its size. It looked like twice the size of the house that they just left in Westwood. The front was all white with large windows. A large, red front door looked inviting with its gold trim.

The driveway they had parked in was red brick and covered the front of the property. It looked less like a driveway and more like a parking lot. There was a large cement wall around the property. The only way in was through a large iron gate, which was left open for them. Katie noticed a "For Sale" sign when they pulled in.

Katie and Sara got out of the car and met Maggie near the front door.

"Sure." Katie laughed.

"What?" Maggie asked, almost in disbelief.

"There is absolutely no way that we can afford this. Plus, we're just looking to rent, and there's a "For Sale" sign out front."

"Don't let any of that scare you," Maggie said. "I have a plan for all of this."

Maggie wasn't forthcoming with the plan, so Katie was sure she just wanted them to go inside and see the house first.

"We're going in there," Sara said. "I've been inside one of these Beverly Hills mansions."

Maggie laughed, "Oh honey. This isn't a mansion. But it's a nice starter home."

Katie agreed in her mind with Sara. It looked like a mansion to her.

Maggie pushed open the front door, and they were immediately met with a rush of cool air. The house was empty, but it was expansive. The entryway led into an open space that looked to double as a living room, family room, kitchen, and dining room. At one point, walls and light fixtures were placed, and the space was designed, but it was tough for Katie to tell what was what at this point.

They strolled along the open spaces, and Maggie pointed out which space was which, but Katie loved looking at it as a blank canvas. It was up to her imagination, and the possibilities felt endless.

Maggie walked them to the back of the house, where the kitchen had mostly been gutted. There were just a few cabinets and a large stove left to identify the space. Katie was about to take a look around when she gazed out of the solid glass back walls.

Just outside the glass was a beautiful outdoor living space. There was a trellis and a large built-in stainless-steel grille. Just beyond that space was the glistening of a large, glass-like pool. Katie walked over to the wall of windows and stared out.

"I told you that you were going to love this place," Maggie gushed.

"Katie, this place is amazing," Sara agreed.

"There are 5 bedrooms upstairs, 3 full baths, a loft area. There's also another bathroom down here and a den, which I can show you."

"This is way too much," Katie said, keeping her eyes on the backyard. She didn't even believe the words as they were coming out of her mouth. "It's just Stephen and I."

"This is a house you can grow into," Maggie said convincingly.

Katie broke her gaze and looked at Maggie. It was almost as though she snapped out of it. She felt something in the pit of her stomach that made it turn sour.

"There's no way we're going to be able to afford this anyway. Plus, we're not looking to buy."

Maggie chimed in. "I know the owner. They are very motivated to get this off of the market. They're going through a terribly messy divorce, and they just want to be done with it. I think I could convince them to do a rent-to-own. That way, you can rent for a year, try it out, and they buy afterward if you decide you want to stay."

Katie thought about it for a minute. His mind was saying yes, but she couldn't get rid of this terrible feeling in the pit of her stomach. It began to grow, and quickly, it was almost full-blown nausea.

"That might work, but how much does this cost? I still don't think there's any way we can afford this," Katie blurted out.

She clutched her stomach a little. Sara looked on to see how Maggie was going to react.

Maggie put her arm around Katie and pulled her off to the corner of the room. She spoke softly so Sara couldn't hear.

"Katie, I've been in this business a long time. I've grown up with people in the film business all of my life. I know that this deal that Stephen got isn't going to be a one-time offer. He's going to direct another and another and another for years to come. The salary is going to grow for each one of them. Sure, you can rent one of those middle-of-the-road houses in Westwood, but you're really going to want to be here in the middle of the action in Beverly Hills."

Katie's look changed. She did want to do what was right for Stephen's career.

"I don't know what Stephen got for this project, but let me tell you, if it's anything over a million, we can get you into this house comfortably."

Katie looked at her. It was double that.

"Maggie, he got —"

Before she could finish, Katie felt a wave of nausea come over her. It was so strong and came on so suddenly that the was nothing she could do. She quickly turned away from Maggie and vomited all over the shiny marble floor.

Maggie jumped back suddenly to avoid being hit.

Sara looked on from the other side of the room. "I guess that means she likes it?"

***

Katie sat on the edge of the bed with the telephone receiver pressed against her ear. She sat perched on the corner and alert. The phone rang and rang as she waited for someone to pick up. She looked at the alarm clock on the nightstand. It said 10:02 PM.

"Come on, Stephen," Katie wailed into the phone. Her knee shook a little as she was waiting for him to pick up. She had the phone cord wrapped around her index finger as she held the receiver. She fiddled with something else in her left hand.

The fifth ring came and went. Then came the sixth. Katie was itching to talk to Stephen, and every ring shot through her like a dagger.

Katie was about to hang up after the eighth ring when she heard a click and a familiar voice on the other end.

"Hello?" Stephen said.

"Hi," she said, with anxiety in her voice.

"Hey, sorry. I just got back to my room. It's been a long day of shooting."

"That's okay," she said. "How did the first day go?"

"Great," Stephen said. "We started with a few easy dialogue scenes so that everyone could get warmed up before we move into actions and stunts in a few days."

"That sounds great," Katie said. Her voice was distant and distracted.

"What's happening there?" Stephen asked. "Did you find us a house yet?"

"Yes," she said. "Maggie has been taking us everywhere these last few days. Sara's been great to help me out and go with me."

"You found one you like? Tell me about it."

"Yeah, it is a really great one."

"Is it in Westwood or Brentwood?" Stephen asked.

"Well, that's just the thing." Katie paused. "It's in neither."

"Don't tell me it's in West Hollywood? You told me you never want to go back there." Stephen was only half joking.

"No." Katie hesitated. She knew she had to just blurt it out. "It's actually in Beverly Hills."

"Beverly Hills!" Stephen exclaimed. "I get one directing job and you're already dreaming big."

"Maggie worked out all of the details for us. She really thinks it's going to work for us. She said it's the best place for us to be to network and meet people if you're going to continue to direct."

"Oh," Stephen said. "Maggie said all of that, did she?"

"Yes," Katie replied. "I know it's a house that you're going to love too."

"I bet." Stephen laughed. "Is it a price tag I'm going to love, though?"

"Well, let's talk about it," Katie said calmly. "There's also something else we have to talk about."

She looked down at her left hand. She was holding a pregnancy test. And the results were positive.

5

January 18th, 1994

Katie closed her eyes and took a deep breath. She tried to calm herself before she got out of bed and ran to the nursery for the third time since she tried to get some sleep. She could hear the baby crying from the other room. He had only been home from the hospital for a little over two weeks, and there had already been a regular schedule of getting up every hour on the hour.

She felt Stephen stir in the bed next to her as she pushed herself up from the bed and lumbered half-asleep out of their bedroom and down the long hallway to the nursery. She tried not to wake Stephen, but she was sure he was awake too.

Katie stumbled her way into the nursery, guided only by a small night light in the far corner of the room. She approached the crib as the crying grew louder and louder in her ear. She reached down and pulled the baby out of the crib and into her arms. She walked slowly to the rocking chair next to the crib and plopped down, careful to support the baby.

"Jakey baby," she cooed. "What's wrong?"

She began rocking back and forth in the chair, and the baby slowly began to calm down. The cries became softer, and there were gaps of silence between them.

It had been a long two weeks since they brought Jake home from the hospital. She went into labor on New Year's Day and, after 18 hours of labor, gave birth to Jake on January 2nd. They stayed in the hospital overnight and arrived back home on January 3rd.

Katie wasn't prepared for what came next. She knew she was going to be tired all the time, but she wasn't fully prepared for the feedings every two hours. The endless diaper changes. The changes to her body she wasn't even yet fully aware of.

She looked down at Jake. She was so proud of her baby boy, whose blue eyes looked just like his father's. He looked back at her briefly before closing his eyes again and calming down.

"Katie, please!" Stephen's voice startled her as she jerked, and Jake started crying again.

"What?" she asked as she looked up and saw Stephen standing in the doorway.

"Why is he crying this time?" Stephen looked just as exhausted as Katie.

"Shhhh, baby," Katie said, ignoring Stephen. She looked down at Jake, gripped him a little tighter, and rocked a little faster.

"I have a day full of meetings tomorrow, and I really need to get some sleep. The car arrives at 5 AM to take me to the studio," Stephen moaned.

Katie tried not to roll her eyes. "I'm sorry, Stephen. Babies cry. I'm trying to calm him down."

Stephen was having a hard time balancing work and a baby at home. Even though Katie took care of the baby, Stephen hadn't yet adjusted to the baby's schedule. Katie was exhausted, but she didn't mind the multiple feedings a night. She felt a closeness to the baby. It was something she had never felt before.

"I'm going back to bed," Stephen said, lumbering out of the room.

Katie looked down again at Jake. He started to calm down again after Stephen left the room. She smiled at him and rocked him back to sleep.

***

Stephen awoke the next morning before the crack of dawn. Katie was sleeping in the bed next to him, and he could hear silence coming from the baby monitor next to her head. He quietly left the bed and went into the bathroom to shower.

Afterward, he quickly got dressed and made his way to the kitchen, trying not to wake anyone in the house. He made himself a cup of coffee, downed it in just a few sips, and left the house.

He hopped into his Mercedes and made his way from Beverly Hills to the studio.

When he pulled into his designated parking spot, he took a deep breath before exiting the car. Having a child was much more for him than he had expected. He was enjoying his newfound success in the film industry. Variety was touting him as the next Martin Scorsese.

His first film was a hit, and he was the talk of the town. He had his pick of any project that he wanted. He wanted to throw himself into his work and live up to his new reputation.

He was finding that harder and harder each day with a new baby. The constant interruptions every night meant that he wasn't able to get any sleep. He was hardly sleeping before this as it was. Five hours was a good night for him. Now, he was lucky if he could sleep even two hours straight without being woken up.

That was causing him problems at work. He couldn't concentrate and people noticed him drifting off in meetings. It wasn't a good look to meet with the producers of his upcoming film and they find him nodding off in the middle of the meeting.

He was really stressed about today. Today, they were casting for the leading lady in his film. This was the fourth day of casting, and they hadn't found any viable candidates yet. The casting directors on this film were letting him down.

His first film was virtually cast for him by the time he was brought on as director. With the second, he took a more hands-off approach and allowed the producers to have a large say in casting. This time though, was going to be different. He had the final word in everything from the script to the set to the actors. This was going to be the first film that he made that he truly felt was his.

He couldn't let the baby get in the way of that.

He hopped out of the car and made the short walk to his office on the studio lot. He threw his stuff down on his desk and collapsed into his chair. He looked down at his watch. It was 7:42 AM. No one else would be in until closer to 9 AM. The casting session wasn't scheduled to start until 10 AM, which usually meant closer to 11. That gave Stephen a few hours to get some work done before a parade of actresses tried their hardest to make an impression on him.

That's exactly what happened a few hours later when the casting session started. Stephen sat behind a long table with half a dozen other people. There were casting directors and producers with him. He made sure he sat directly in the center so those around him all knew he was in charge.

As casting assistants brought actress after actress into the room, Stephen began to get discouraged, even bored. They had been doing this for so many days now and haven't even come close to finding the right person for the role.

He needed someone with a fire in her eyes. Someone who could be soft and gentle at times but could take control at other times. That's what the role called for. Nearly everyone he saw so far could only play one or the other. They were either too soft or too over-the-top aggressive. He needed to see both and sometimes both at once.

The lack of interest of anyone had Stephen starting to mentally remove himself from the situation. He paid less and less attention to each actress. He found his eyes getting heavy. It was partially lack of sleep, partially boredom, and partially being seated for too long. He didn't even realize that he had drifted off into sleep during one of the auditions.

The actress came and went, and Stephen didn't hear or say a word. He didn't notice the hush that came over the room after she left. All of the casting directors, assistants, and producers had their eyes fixed on Stephen. He was none the wiser as he grabbed a much-needed respite from the pressures of work and home.

"Um, Stephen," one of the casting directors finally managed to blurt out.

Stephen jerked to life. He noticed the room staring at him, and his face grew flush. The casting director sensed this and decided to continue. "Are you ready to see the next audition?"

"Yes," Stephen blurted out.

The room relaxed, and averted eye contact with Stephen. They were going to continue and pretend like nothing happened.

He was more than happy to go along with that. The next actress who entered the audition room caught Stephen's eye. He couldn't tell if it was because he was being more self-conscious about it or if she really did have something special.

"Hello," she said. She was standing about eight feet in front of the table. She had long, curly brown hair and hazel eyes. She had long legs and was wearing a short skirt that showed them off. She stood straight up and looked Stephen in the eye with purpose. He could feel her energy.

"Hello," Stephen said, not blinking.

"Should I just go ahead and start?" She asked.

"How about we start with your name," he asked. The casting director handed Stephen a headshot and resume. He looked down and saw her name.

"Leah Bennett."

"Hello, Leah," Stephen said, looking back up at her.

She began her audition and Stephen lost himself in it. She was everything he was looking for. She was engaging, commanding, and could be vulnerable.

Stephen didn't even look around the room to read everyone else's temperature. After she finished, he immediately stood up and said, "You've got it."

Leah screamed and ran over to Stephen. She leaned over the table and hugged him. He leaned in and hugged her back. He didn't notice everyone else in the room with their jaws on the floor.

"We'll call your agent and get a deal worked out," Stephen said to her.

"Thank you so much. You won't regret it. I'm so excited." Leah said as she bounced out of the room.

Stephen looked around the room as everyone just stared blankly at him.

"Looks like we're done here," he said. He got up and walked out of the room and back to his office.

Before he could even sit in his chair, one of the producers followed him back to his office. The producer, Harris Goldberg, was a man much older than Stephen. He was in his mid-50s and had been producing films for the studio for twenty years. He was not a particularly imposing man, but he could be forceful when he had to. And this was going to be one of those times.

"Get out of here, Harris," Stephen said.

"Excuse me?" Harris said.

"I don't need you in my office right now. I have work to do."

Harris ignored him. "What was that stunt that you just pulled back there?"

Stephen feigned innocence. "What stunt?"

"Do you know what you just did?"

"Yes," Stephen said, his voice quivering slightly as he tried to remain strong. "We were having a casting session for the lead actress. I hired a lead actress. Wasn't that the point of what we were trying to do here?"

"You know this is a collaborative process," Harris reminded him.

"Oh, fuck that," Stephen said.

Harris had heard it all before. "You know you can't just go rogue like that and hire whoever you want. The producers want a say. The casting people want a say. The studio has to have the final say."

"No," Stephen said. "That's where you're wrong. This is my film, and I'm going to have the final say."

"Were you embarrassed because we caught you sleeping back there? Was that what that was?"

"I don't know what the hell you're talking about."

"Listen, Stephen. We all understand this is only your third film. You have a newborn at home. That's a lot of responsibility."

"I can handle the responsibility just fine, Harris." Stephen grew angrier with each word.

"I will do what I can to smooth this over with the studio, but can I give you some advice?"

Stephen didn't look open to hearing it, but Harris continued anyway.

"You don't want to piss the studio off. You want to play the game by their rules. They're the ones with the money. They're the ones with the influence that determines if you ever get a job in this town again. You have to make sure they support your decisions. If they don't, they'll shut you down or replace you.

"You're on a hot streak," Harris continued. "Let's keep it that way."

Stephen began to calm down a little.

"Fine, go do what you need to do with the studio. But I want Leah as the lead in this film."

Harris looked at him, trying not to roll his eyes. "This is the hill you're going to die on?"

"Look, everyone in that room needs to know that this is my film. I was chosen to direct this, I earned it, and this is going to be my film. Everyone will remember that now."

"Fine," Harris said. "If that's the way you're going to play this. But, please. Remember what I said."

Stephen turned and sat in his chair as Harris made his way out of the room. Stephen seethed as he put his feet up on his desk. Who was Harris to tell him what to do? This was his film. The studio picked him to direct, and he wasn't going to let outside interference get in the way of making his masterpiece.

He wasn't going to let anything stand in the way of his career.

6

March 16th, 2002

Katie woke up refreshed before her alarm even went off. She rolled over and turned it off, and Stephen was still fast asleep next to her. She carefully slipped out of bed. She didn't want to wake up Stephen. It was a few minutes before 8:30 a.m., and his alarm wasn't due to go off until 9 a.m.

She showered quickly and blow-dried her hair. Then, she pulled it back into a quick ponytail and slipped into her workout clothes. She slipped out of the bathroom and was heading down to the kitchen when she heard Stephen's alarm go off.

Katie bounced down to the kitchen where she could smell coffee already brewing. She was loving their new house.

They moved only a few months ago, and this house was nearly triple the size of the last one. After Stephen's third and fourth films both made over 100 million dollars, they decided that money was no object and that they should splurge on the best house they could find.

Katie found it quickly. One of her hobbies had been keeping tabs on Beverly Hills real estate, and she knew exactly what she was looking for. She was no longer content with just living in Beverly Hills; she knew she wanted to be in Beverly Hills Flats. She convinced Stephen that money was no object, and she waited for just the right place to come up.

She wasn't concerned with the actual house; she was more than happy to do renovations. She wanted a good location. She was very surprised that only weeks after they decided to pull the trigger, a house that met all of her qualifications came onto the market.

The house, perched on Calle Vista Drive, was designed by renowned architect Richard Lowry and had only been lived in for two years before the owner decided to put it on the market.

It was love at first sight for Katie. The house was a Mediterranean-style mansion with seven bedrooms and nine bathrooms. It stood perched on an alcove and offered spectacular city and ocean views. It made Katie feel like she was sitting on top of the world, and she was the queen.

Directly inside the two double front doors were two large marble staircases. At the top, they met and offered entry to the second level. Between the two staircases was a large crystal chandelier that easily cost more than five years of Katie's old waitress salary.

Under the chandelier, a hallway led to the first level of the house. There was a study, formal dining and living rooms, two bathrooms, and a kitchen that was nearly 1,500 square feet on its own.

The entire back half of the house was sold glass, looking out onto an infinity pool and a view of the ocean in the distance. This view wasn't available to all of Beverly Hills, but Katie loved how elite it made her feel.

The floor of the house was entirely marble, and no detail had been overlooked. It was almost as if the designer of the house was in Katie's brain and designing everything for her.

At the top of the dual staircases was a long hallway that led to the seven bedrooms and five of the bedrooms. Katie and Stephen's master bedroom was at the end of the hall.

It had dual doors that opened into a room that was nearly 1,000 square feet. Each bedroom had its own walk-in closet and a private master bathroom with a soaking tub in front of a window that offered an even better view than the back patio.

The other six bedrooms lined the hallway between the master bedroom and the staircase. Some had their own private bathrooms, and one bathroom was in the hallway but not connected to any bedroom.

Katie grabbed a mug that had already been placed on the counter for her and poured herself a cup of coffee. She liked it strong, black, and hot and immediately took a sip as soon as her mug was full.

She stood alone in the kitchen, enjoying the silence. That was another one of her favorite things about the new house. Even if people were stirring in other parts of the house, she could never hear them. She relished the quiet, and this house gave it to her in spades.

Even though she couldn't hear it, she knew that people were moving around in other parts of the house. A lot had changed for Katie over the last few years. Stephen was around less and less as his career grew bigger and bigger.

He moved on from directing and began producing, which meant he was spending much more time on each project. He would spend 16 hours a day at his office on the studio lot, leaving Katie at home. She had gotten used to seeing him only for a few minutes in the morning and a few before bed. If he even came in before Katie went to bed. That was never a given.

That left Katie at home most of the time, so she started branching out. She met another group of Beverly Hills moms and threw herself into being a perfect Beverly Hills wife. She would spend a few hours a day working out, lunch with her friends, and spend a lot of time shopping so that she would have the perfect wardrobe and they would have the perfect house.

She became more interested in interior design and spent time working on making changes in the house — nothing foundational, just redecorating rooms and finding just the right pieces of furniture.

This kept her busy during the day. She wasn't sure she had found the purpose in life she was always seeking, but there were definitely worse ways her life could have ended.

Katie's streak of silence was broken by a happy, piercing scream. It grew louder as it came down the stairs and made its way back to the kitchen, where Katie was still standing. It was Jake. Narrowly behind him was his nanny, Elizabeth.

She was a few years younger than Katie and stood a few inches taller. Her hair was wavy and nearly pitch back. His skin was porcelain white with the cleanest complexion that Katie had ever seen. No matter what time of day it was or how long she had been chasing after Jake, Katie had never seen her looking anything more than 100% together.

They hired Elizabeth when Jake was about a year old. He was now eight, and Katie was so happy she'd stuck with them through the years. Jake adored her, and it was a huge help for Katie to have her. She did all of the baths, reading time, school drop-offs and pick-ups, soccer practices, and all of the things that Katie didn't have time to do.

"Hi, Baby," Katie said as Jake ran over and hugged her leg.

She nearly spilled coffee on his head from the jerk.

"Easy, baby," she said, taking another sip.

"Come on, Jakey," Elizabeth said. "Let's get your breakfast ready."

Katie gave a small smile and nod to Elizabeth and she replied with the same.

Elizabeth maneuvered around the large kitchen island and sat Jake on a bar stool on the other side. Katie stood there as Jake talked away, sipping her coffee. She pretended she was still in silence.

She closed her eyes as she sipped the steaming coffee and took deep breaths.

"What do you want today, Jakey?" Elizabeth asked.

"Trix! Trix! Trix!" Jake chanted.

"You got it!" Elizabeth smiled and walked to the pantry. She opened the door, walked inside, and retrieved the box of cereal.

Before she could even pour it, there was some shuffling coming down the stairs again. Katie looked down at her watch. It was Saturday and only 8:30 AM. There was no way it was Stephen already. He didn't arrive home until long past midnight last night, so he'd be in bed for a few more hours trying to decompress after a long week.

That means it must be...

"Good Morning, Everyone," a voice nearly shouted.

It was Stacey, their other nanny. Stacey was always a little over the top. Physically, she looked very similar to Elizabeth: tall and thin, with dark hair and perfect skin. But where Elizabeth knew her place in the family, Stacey had only been with them for about three months and was still figuring things out.

Stacey held Jessica in her arms. Jessica was just four months old. Katie knew when she was pregnant with Jessica that she needed a second nanny immediately. She raised Jake by herself for the first year but didn't have the strength to do it for a second baby.

She survived the first few weeks with night nurses and Elizabeth's help during the day. They found Stacey about a month after Jessica was born. She started a few weeks later, and it was a weight off of Katie's shoulders.

Stacey hopped with Jessica in her arms over to Katie.

"Good Morning, Mommy," Stacey cooed in a baby voice as she bounced up and down next to Katie.

Katie took Jessica's tiny hand in hers, gave it a little squeeze, and smiled at her. Stacey bounced happily around the kitchen with the baby, carefully maneuvering around Elizabeth as she poured milk and Trix into a bowl.

Katie took one final sip of her mostly full mug of coffee and set it down on the counter. She needed some more quiet.

"I'll be downstairs if anyone needs me," she said. She made her way to the far side of the kitchen, where there was a large wooden door. She opened the door and descended the staircase to disappear into the lowest level of the house.

While it was technically the basement, Katie always called it the lower level of the house. There was nothing about it that was basement-like.

It was divided into three separate areas. Directly at the bottom of the stairs, you could either go left or right. To the right was where Katie spent most of her time. There was a sprawling gym with more equipment than Katie could even use. Quite frankly, she didn't know what much of it did and typically stuck to the elliptical. Beyond the gym was a full-sized indoor swimming pool and a sauna.

When she bought the house, Katie was most excited about the indoor pool. Although southern California had great weather, she could picture the house full of kids running and jumping in the pool all year round.

Katie typically spent her mornings working out, swimming laps, and relaxing in the sauna before showering again for the second time of the day.

To the left of the stairs was an area almost as large, but one that Katie didn't typically visit. Stephen had set up a large screening room before they moved in. It had a floor-to-ceiling screen and three rows of recliner chairs that held a group of about 18.

Behind the chairs, there was a small projection box on the wall that held the projector for the screen. Katie didn't know too much about it, but Stephen said it was state-of-the-art. He'd only spent a few nights down here since they moved in and Katie often wondered if it was even worth the money they spent on it.

On the far side of the screening room was another door. That door led to a storage area where they kept random odds and ends. It was a fully finished space, but they didn't keep much in there. There was also a door in that room that led outside to the back part of the house. This was the entrance that the pool company used. They kept all of the pool chemicals in there and could easily access either the indoor or outdoor pools from there.

Katie took a right at the bottom of the stairs and headed to the gym. She grabbed a bottle of water out of a small fridge on the floor and hopped onto an elliptical. She began pedaling while thinking about her itinerary for the day.

She had a brunch planned with the girls at 1 PM. If it were anything like their normal Saturday afternoon brunches, it would likely extend beyond the afternoon and into the early evening.

They could spend all afternoon drinking mimosas and laughing. The brunches and lunches with her gals were often Katie's favorite parts of the week. Stephen would be home trying to decompress from a long week at the studio, and it was often better if she was out of his hair anyway. This allowed him to spend some of his free time alone, and he could conjure up the energy he would need to make it through another tough week.

Katie looked around as she exercised. She loved the lower level of the house. There was always peace and quiet down here. This was her place of respite. She knew what was going on above her. Stephen would be getting up soon. Jake would be running wild. Jessica would need to be changed. The nannies had control of all of that.

She could spend all the time she wanted downstairs in silence with her thoughts.

7

December 1st, 2015

The entire house was buzzing. Music was coming from a live band outside near the pool. All of the kitchen windows were wide open. The music poured into the house and echoed across the marble.

The pool area was crowded with people. Katie stood in the center. She was the hostess today and was the perfect Beverly Hills wife. There were serving stations, tables, balloons, flower arrangements, and servers everywhere. Katie spared no expense for this party. Even though it was a December day, it was unseasonably warm in Beverly Hills, and Katie was grateful. She was able to have the party outdoors.

She and Stephen mingled with couples and singles. Everyone appeared to be over the age of 40. Looking around the room was similar to seeing a fashion show. Women were decked out in their most elegant gowns and dresses. Men were almost exclusively in tuxedos.

It certainly didn't look like a child's birthday party, but that's what it was. Jessica, the birthday girl, was sat inside on barstool in the kitchen. She stared blankly at her phone, everyone once responding to a message.

Her foot swung from the barstool unconsciously to the rhythm of the music pouring in from the open windows.

"Hey, birthday girl," she heard a voice yell. She looked up to see Leah Bennett entering the room.

"Oh, hey," Jessica mustered unenthusiastically.

"Oh no," Leah said. "I know that tone. What's up?"

Jessica looked up at her, and Leah took a seat in the barstool next to her.

"Nothing," Jessica insisted.

Leah looked through the kitchen windows at the very adult party going on outside.

"Can I tell you a story?" Leah asked.

"Sure," Jessica said. She looked up from her phone and gave Leah her full attention.

"When I was just about your age, I wanted nothing more than the Grease Soundtrack on vinyl. You're probably too young to know what a record even is."

Jessica smiled at her. "I know what they are. We have some packed away down in the basement. I just get my music on my phone."

"Yes." Leah chuckled. "Everything is so easy nowadays. You have everything you want at

72

your fingertips. But that wasn't the case back when I was younger."

"That sucks," Jessica said.

"Well, we didn't know any better back then. So, I told my mom over and over that I wanted the Grease album for my birthday. I used to sit around for hours waiting for any song I liked to come on the radio.

"Didn't they have Spotify back then? Or iTunes?"

"No." Leah smiled. "We had to wait. Well, when the big day finally came, I was so excited that I could have a party with my friends."

"Yeah," Jessica said. "You got to have a party with your friends."

Jessica looked out the window at the adults and not a kid in sight. Leah smiled back at her.

"Yes, I was lucky. But, when it came time to unwrap my presents, I was in for a surprise."

"What was that?" Jessica asked.

"Well, I had this very flat rectangle present. I knew it had to be a record album. I was so excited that when I was allowed to open my presents, I tore into it first. It had to be what I told my mother I wanted a hundred times."

"Did you get what you wanted?" Jessica asked.

"Much to my horror, when I tore off the wrapping, it was the Saturday Night Fever soundtrack."

"What's that?" Jessica asked, puzzled.

Leah laughed. "Well, let's just say my mom bought me the wrong thing for my birthday."

"Ugh," Jessica grunted.

"Exactly. I had only told her a thousand times, but she bought the wrong one."

"Weren't you so disappointed? Aren't mothers supposed to know what their children want?"

"Well, I'm not going to lie. I was very disappointed. I could have thrown a fit right there and could have pouted or yelled at her."

"What did you do?" Jessica asked.

"I went over and gave my mom a hug and thanked her," Leah said.

"Why would you do something like that? She couldn't even get your present right."

"Because she tried. Very hard." Leah said. "You see, my dad wasn't in the picture like your dad is. My mom had to fight and save for everything we got as a kid. I knew that If I told my mom that the present was wrong would just make her feel bad."

"But it was wrong," Jessica protested.

"Yes," Leah said. "It was the wrong present, but my mother cared so much that she tried to get me the right thing, but just made a mistake. I had a choice that I could make. I could choose anger about it. Or I could choose love. So, I chose love. And I've been making that my mantra ever since. Every single time I'm in a tough situation, I think about love. What would it mean in this situation to choose love? Then I do it!"

"I would still be mad if my present was wrong," Jessica said.

Leah laughed at her. "The good news is, that with the money I got for my birthday, I was able to buy myself the right present. I got what I wanted, and my mom got to be happy. Everyone was happy in that situation."

"I guess that makes sense," Jessica begrudgingly agreed.

"So, let me ask you a question," Leah said. "I know this isn't the party that you wanted. But what if you chose love in this situation? What would that look like?"

"Probably going over to my mother, giving her a hug, and thanking her for the party," Jessica said, unsure.

"Exactly." Leah smiled.

"And then sneaking out of the party and going to see your friends, which is what you really want," a voice from behind them said. They turned around to see Jake standing there.

Jessica smiled at her brother.

"I'm out of here for this part of the discussion." Leah smiled. She hopped off of the barstool and looked at Jessica one more time. Jessica noticed the warmth in her eyes and smiled back at her.

Jake walked over and sat on the barstool on the other side of Jessica as Leah exited the room and headed back to the party. Jessica turned to face Jake.

"What are you talking about? Mom will kill me if I leave."

"Jess, come on," Jake said. "Look around out there."

They both looked out the windows at the party outside. Katie was still floating around the crowd, making small talk with a cocktail in her hand.

"Do you really think Mom is going to notice if you're gone?" Jake asked.

"Probably not," Jessica confessed.

"Where would you rather be right now?" Jake asked.

"Besides Hawaii?" Jessica laughed.

"We can go there if you want," Jake deadpanned.

"No, no, no." She slapped him on the knee.

"I'll drive you. And…" He paused. "If, for some reason, Mom notices you're missing, I'll cover for you."

"Hold on," Jessica said, turning to her phone. She typed a message, waited, then typed another.

Jake looked on patiently while his sister made plans with her friends.

"Ok, we're all going to meet at Ashleigh's house," Jessica said.

"Oh, that's in Brentwood, right?" Jake asked.

"Yes," Jessica answered.

"Let's go," Jake said.

Within minutes, they were in Jake's car and on their way to Brentwood. Jake navigated his way through the streets and Jessica chose songs from her phone to play.

"Thank you, Jake," Jessica said.

"What are big brothers for?" he asked.

"Did you hear that speech Leah gave me about choosing love?" Jessica was curious how much Jake had heard.

"Yeah," he said. "That was a really nice story."

"I don't know if I would be strong enough to do that," Jessica confessed.

"What do you mean? You're one of the strongest people I know," Jake said confidently as he slowed for a red light.

"Maybe strong enough isn't the right term. Maybe I mean forgiving enough," Jessica said, unsure.

They sat in silence, Jessica's music playing in the background, until the light turned green. Jake hit the gas pedal, and they were back on the road again.

"I think the moral of what she was saying is very good, though, don't you?" He asked his little sister.

"Yes," she said. "I get it. Things aren't always going to go right, so we should choose to make the best of it."

"Exactly," Jake said. "I think that's what she was getting at."

"But—" Jessica paused. "What if I can't? What if I can't always make the best of every situation? What if I can't, as she put it, choose love?"

"I think it's a learning curve for all of us," Jake said. "The only thing we can really do is to strive to be better every day."

"I think that's a good way of looking at it," Jessica said, satisfied with her brother's answer.

"Who all are you meeting?" Jake asked, changing the subject.

"Ashleigh is going to be there. I think Chelsea, too. They invited Mason, but I'm not sure if he'll come or not."

"Mason?" Jake asked.

"Yeah," Jessica said, retreating into her seat a little.

"Isn't he a little old to be hanging out with 13-year-old girls?" Jake said.

"He's kind of dating Chelsea," Jessica said.

"He's almost my age." Jake was shocked.

"She likes to date older guys," Jessica said flatly.

"Just please, promise me, you won't be looking up to her as a role model."

Jessica laughed. "Oh, please, Jake. I'm 13. I can make my own decisions."

Jake pulled the car into a driveway in Brentwood.

"We're here," Jake said.

"Thank you for bringing me," Jessica said.

"How are you going to get home?" Jake asked.

"I'll ask Ashleigh's mom for a ride. Or Mason," Jessica joked.

"Very funny," Jake said.

Jessica opened the car door, but Jake stopped her before she could get out.

"What?" She asked, looking back at him.

"I have something for you," Jake said. "You can consider it a birthday present."

Jessica sat back in her seat and smiled at him.

Jake reached into his pocket and pulled out a small model skateboard about 4 inches long. He handed it to Jessica.

"A Tech Deck?" Jessica asked. "How retro of you."

"This was my favorite toy when I was a kid. I used to carry it around with me everywhere I went."

"Great," Jessica said, almost rolling her eyes.

"It's not just any Tech Deck," Jake said. He slid the front off of the skateboard to reveal a hidden compartment below. Inside was a key.

"What?" Jessica said, smiling. "What's that?"

"It's a key to the door in the storage room in the basement. When I used to sneak off when I was a teenager, I was able to sneak back into the house by using the door in the basement. There's no camera in that room, and there's no alarm on the door, so you can get in undetected."

Jessica smiled and grabbed the miniature skateboard from him. "This is awesome, thank you."

She reached across the car and gave her brother a huge hug. He hugged back but didn't let go. "I want you to remember something."

"What's that?" Jessica asked. He let her go, and she fell back into her seat.

"I'm your big brother. I am always here for you. This key is more than just a key. I want you to know that no matter how you are feeling. If you're mad at mom or you're mad at dad. I'm here for you, and I'm always going to support you no matter what. To steal Leah's words, that's how I'll choose love. I'm going to be your big brother and always here for you."

"Thank you," Jessica said. She gave him another hug.

"That entire speech, and all I get is a thank you?"

"Yes." Jessica laughed. "You'll always be my dorky big brother."

Jake laughed. "Get out of here now. Let me know how sneaking back in goes."

Jessica jumped out of the car and shut the door behind her. She ran toward Ashleigh's house but paused about halfway there to look back at her brother. He was waiting until she got in the house okay.

She couldn't articulate it at the time, but she was grateful for his support. She had always felt close to her brother, and this moment was only going to bring them closer.

***

A few days later, Jessica arrived home from school. She was feeling pretty good. With her brother's help, she had successfully snuck out of the house, and exactly as he had predicted, no one noticed.

She fully expected her dad or even her mother to say something about her disappearance, but neither seemed to notice. She now proudly carried around the Tech Deck with the hidden key.

For the last two days, she has used the key on the side entrance of the house to sneak in and practice. She is feeling herself and wants to push the boundaries of what she can get away with.

She stood in front of the side door, pulled the Tech Deck out of her pocket, and grabbed the key from inside of it. She put it in the lock and pushed the door open into the storage area. The room wasn't particularly well air-conditioned, and Jessica was always struck by how hot and stuffy the air was inside. It also smelled of chlorine. This is where the pool company kept all of the pool chemicals for both the indoor and outdoor pools, so the smell was heavy.

She turned on the lights and made her way through the storage room to the other side. When she got to the other side of the room, she turned off another light switch and the lights in the room quickly darkened. She pulled open the door that led into the screening room, and light flooded into the now-darkened storage room. She stepped into the screening room and shut the door behind her.

She immediately noticed something different. There was way too much light downstairs. Usually, only a few dim lights were on, but today, the basement was completely bathed in light.

As Jessica's eyes adjusted to the bright lights, she also heard unfamiliar sounds. It took her a moment to comprehend, but she heard a loud whirling noise and several deep male voices.

She slowly stepped out of the screening room and saw movement across the basement from the indoor pool area. She quickly hopped over to the bottom of the stairs and stood on the last one. She peered around the corner into the pool area, and she saw her mother standing there in front of the pool, pointing and directing.

She watched from a distance for a moment when Katie happened to glance over and see her peering out from the staircase.

"Jessica," Katie said, surprised. "I didn't even hear you come down the stairs."

Jessica was relieved. She managed to sneak in again, this time with her mother in the basement, and she still didn't notice. She stepped off of the staircase and walked over to her mother.

As she walked into the pool area, she saw what was happening. Katie was standing in front of a group of workers from the pool company. They were draining the pool.

"Mom?" She asked, confused. "What are you doing?"

"I'm draining the pool," she said.

"Why?" Jessica was genuinely confused.

"You kids don't use it anymore; it's just down here costing us money. There's no reason to keep it."

"What brought this on?" Jessica said.

"It's something I've been thinking about for a while now," Katie said. Her attention was focused on the pool workers and not on her daughter. Jessica was used to it and barely noticed.

"Oh, okay, Mom." Jessica waited for a response that never came. Katie was too focused on the workers.

"I'm going to head back upstairs then," Jessica said.

"Bye," Katie said flatly.

Jessica walked out of the room, and Katie continued to stare at the pool as the water slowly receded.

What she said to Jessica was the truth. She had been thinking about the pool a lot lately. She thought about what the pool represented to her. She remembered buying the house and loving that it came with both an indoor and outdoor pool. She could have fun with her family year-round and didn't have to think about the weather.

Katie remembered her childhood in the Midwest. They always found ways to have fun, but she always loved swimming. Her mother said she was like a fish; she spent so much time in the water. Katie hated the winters. They couldn't swim in the pool or the nearby pond. It seemed so long and cold and Katie wanted the summers to never end. That's part of what drew her to Los Angeles in the first place. The promise of one long summer.

Now, one of the things she longed for most as a child was to be able to give her children year-round summertime, even if some of it was indoors.

But, for reasons that were clear to Katie, she couldn't have that same relationship with her children. She tried, she did the best she could, but she just didn't have the strength to keep up her perfect Beverly Hills mom persona in public and in private.

So, in private, Katie suffered. This pool reminded her of all of the things that she lost, all of the things that she wanted out of her life that went so wrong, so she decided to have it drained.

It could stand as a reminder made of cold, shiny, hard marble—a feeling that Katie related to every day.

8

November 8th, 2019

It was a beautiful November day. The Los Angeles sun was shining. It wasn't too hot, and it wasn't too cold. It felt like Los Angeles hadn't seen a day like this in years. It was the perfect day for Jake's premiere.

For the last three months, he had been working nonstop seven days a week to finish the film. This included editing, sound editing, re-recording dialogue, and special effects. It felt like a never-ending process, and Jake was glad it was finally coming to an end.

Jake awoke to the light shining through his window. He woke up in the same bedroom he grew up in. He still lived with his parents and his sister. He had been rarely home while he was filming, and it never occurred to him to find his own place.

Jessica was almost 18, and he was sure she would be moving out the first chance she got.

Jake was different, though. He felt his place at home and never had any desire to leave.

He stretched and hopped out of bed. He caught sight of himself in the mirror as he walked by. His hair was way too long and disheveled. He knew he needed to get it cut before the premiere this evening.

Although he was well into his 20s, when he saw himself in the mirror, he felt as if he had never grown out of his awkward teen years. He was tall and thin. His shoulder bones protruded from his skin, and his chest had almost a sunken, hollow look in the middle. His frame was so vertically straight that it looked as if any clothes he had might just slide right off at any point.

He needed to make himself presentable before the evening, so he walked from his room into the adjoining bathroom and hopped in the shower.

He was done moments later and bounced down the stairs. The house hadn't changed much over the years. At least that Jake had noticed, his mother redecorated over the years. It felt like she was always changing the décor, but there hadn't been any major remodeling.

The only construction he could remember in the house was done on the lower level when he was in his early teens. Even then, it was just a blur to him.

As he rounded the bottom of one of the dual staircases, he made his way between them and moved his way to the back of the house. He was surprised to be greeted by his mother. She wasn't usually up this early. He pulled his phone out of his pocket and glanced down at the time. It was 11 AM. He slept longer than he thought.

"Morning, Mom," he said.

Katie stood in the kitchen holding her mug of coffee. Her natural blonde hair had gotten unnaturally blonder as the years went by. Her once glossy and alert green/blue eyes had faded in color. They were closer to hazel now and no longer such a striking feature.

She was in her early 50s but kept her physique. She was a successful Beverly Hills wife and had to keep up with her appearance, which led her to have a few procedures over the years. She never wanted to look completely plastic, so she tried to keep it to fillers and Botox that would wear off over time.

She stood and sipped her strong black coffee. She almost didn't notice that Jake had come into the room.

"Morning, baby," she muttered.

"Now, Mom," he said, walking over to stand next to her. "Don't forget that the limo is going to be here at 6 PM to pick us up."

Katie stood sipping her coffee.

"Mom," Jake said, a little louder this time. Katie looked up at him, and her glassy eyes met his. Jake could tell she wasn't quite awake yet.

"Don't forget, you need to be ready for the limo."

Katie smiled at him. She raised her hand and put it on his cheek. He was a full eight inches taller than her.

"I'll be ready," she said.

"Good. I need to run out and get a haircut and pick up my tux. I will be back around 3 PM. Jess should be home from school by then."

Katie pulled her hand down from his face and put it around the warmth of her mug.

"I'll text Dad to make sure he's home by then, too," Jake said.

Katie took another sip of her coffee.

***

Jake was the first one waiting by the front door at 5:45 p.m. He was so nervous that he couldn't wait any longer to get dressed. He knew it was going to be like pulling teeth to get the rest of the family out of the house on time, but he was going to give it his best shot.

At 5:52 PM, the limo pulled up out front. He looked down at his phone as it alerted him to motion outside. He pulled up the camera app and saw a grid of cameras pop up on his phone. They were everywhere. He had one for the living room and one for the kitchen. There was one marked LL-Pool and LL-Screening room. They were mostly dark. There was another that showed the large back patio and pool area. There was another for the front door. If Jake had scrolled he would have found even more covering most of the grounds and rooms in the house. The only rooms that didn't have cameras were the bedrooms and bathrooms.

Jake pulled up the camera in the driveway and noticed the long black car pull to a stop not far from the front door.

"The limo is here," he yelled up the stairs. The house was so large that no one could hear him.

He reached back down on his phone, pushed a red microphone button on the camera app, and said, "The limo is here."

His voice echoed throughout the house. Every camera was also equipped with a speaker, and he used it as a PA announcement for his family. The only camera upstairs was in the hallway, but Jake knew from experience that the speaker was loud enough to be heard even in the bedrooms.

He waited a few minutes at the bottom of the double staircase. He didn't hear any motion from upstairs. He looked down at his phone again, and the time said 5:55 PM. He would give them a few more minutes before he made his announcement.

When the time changed to 5:57 PM, he noticed movement at the top of the staircases. He looked up to where they met and saw Jessica. She was wearing a long, flowing black dress and looked much older than her 17 years.

"Wow, Jess," he blurted out.

Jess grabbed the handrail and descended the right staircase. She looked uncomfortable in heels, so she firmly held the railing the entire way down.

Jessica looked like the spitting image of her mother at that age. She had bright blue/green eyes and full, straight blonde hair. For tonight, Jess had managed to tame it by pulling it back and up. Several curls fell softly from the back.

Her dress was fitting but not overly revealing. She wasn't the type of teenage girl who liked getting dressed up. Jess marched to the beat of her own drum. She liked to try new things and see what caught her fancy at the moment. She had a wild streak in her and rarely thought things through.

One day, she'd be playing sports with the boys, and the next, she'd be hanging out in the pool with her girlfriends. She had the unique social ability that Katie also had, which allowed her to fit in with everyone. She also had the same desire to find herself that Katie had at her age.

Katie used it to move to Los Angeles and luck her way into becoming a Beverly Hills wife. Jess hadn't given that much thought to what she wanted to do with her life, but she firmly knew she did not want to spend it being a housewife.

As Jess stepped off the last stair, Jake reached out and grabbed Jessica's hand. She grabbed back and used his firm grip to steady herself.

"What do you think?" she said, raising her eyebrows.

"It's perfect," Jake said. "You're going to look great in those red carpet pictures."

He was always very protective of his baby sister. Although they were seven years apart, Jake had never left home, so he had been there the entire time she was going up.

"Thank you," Jess replied. She stood next to Jake and looked down at the time on her phone, which she held in her left hand. "What do you think is the over/under on them being here on time?"

"I wouldn't put any money on them being ready on time. We realistically don't need to leave here until 6:30 PM, but I told them 6:00 PM so they'd be ready."

Jessica laughed. "That's perfect. That's what we need to do all the time." She looked over a Jake. His eyes caught her, and she smiled at him.

"What?" Jake asked, his eyes darting away.

"I still can't believe my big brother made a movie."

"Trust me," Jake said. "Most days, I can't believe it either."

"And based on that urban legend, too," Jess continued.

"I don't know. People seem to think that it's true," Jake said.

"Do you really think that there's some monster out there in the world that would dump a baby in the middle of the desert and just leave it there to die?" Jess was curious.

"Maybe," Jake said. "That rumor has been circulating around school ever since I was a kid."

"Yeah," Jess said. "But, if that many people know about it, don't you think there would be some sort of record about it? Or an arrest? Or people would actually know who did it?"

"Yeah, I guess that's true."

"It's got to be just a stupid thing that people say. You know that all of these kids in Beverly Hills have nothing better to do with their time than to make up stories about each other."

"Oh, I certainly don't miss those days in high school." Jake laughed.

"I can't wait to finish out this year," Jessica said. "Trust me. After this movie premieres is going to dig up a whole new set of rumors. It's kind of like a game of telephone. Pretty soon, it will be someone dumping an alien on Mars or something like that."

Jake laughed again. "Well, look, that old rumor worked out for me. Someone heard it along the way, and Richard wrote a script about it. And now I'm making my debut with it."

Jessica smiled at him. "I'm so happy you got this chance."

"Are you excited about your birthday dinner tomorrow?" Jake asked her.

"Oh, yes. You know, that's how every 18-year-old wants to spend their birthday. Dinner with my family."

"It's fine. It's tradition. I had dinner, snuck out, and partied with my friends on my 18th birthday. I fully expect you to do the same thing."

Jessica laughed. "Oh, you know I'm going to need to get hammered after dinner with Mom and Dad."

***

At exactly 7 PM, the limo pulled up to the red carpet. The scene was completely set for Jake's big debut. The red carpet led down the outside of the theater. It was marked on one side by a long velvet rope and on the backside for advertisements for sponsors and movie posters.

On the other side of the velvet rope were hundreds of reporters, cameramen, paparazzi, and fans, all hoping to get a glimpse of the family. While the movie stars are typically the main event at a premiere, the studio had been hyping up Jake's involvement with the film since they hired him as the director.

It was a "passing of the torch" type of situation between Stephen and Jake. Stephen had started his career by directing and slowly made his way through the industry to become one of the most powerful producers of the day.

The buzz surrounding Jake's directorial debut was that he was going to follow in his father's footsteps. All of the news outlets had been feeding this narrative in the promotion leading up to the film's premiere.

A man in a tuxedo approached the limo door. He opened it, and flashes of light filled the sky. At least 50 photographers must have been standing outside the limo at the edge of the red carpet, ready to take photos of the family.

Jessica stepped out of the limo first. The man in the tuxedo reached down and grabbed her hand. He helped her as she stepped out and balanced herself on her stilettos. She could hear the crowd cheering and reporters talking to their cameras in the background. She heard her name a few times but couldn't hear anything else clearly.

It was also so surreal to her to be in these types of situations. She knew her father was always in the public eye when she was growing up. Now, it was happening again with Jake. One thing was for certain: Jessica knew she wanted no part of this for herself.

She smiled awkwardly and waved to a few fans who stood behind the reporters and cameras. Maybe a few knew she was Jake's sister. She figured most didn't care.

Next, Katie stepped out of the limo, again aided by the man in the tuxedo. She wore a tight, shimmering red gown. It clung to her body and showed off the figure she had worked so hard to keep over the years. Her hair was long and flowing and her makeup was done to perfect. She was the Beverly Hills wife now, like it or not, and she had to look the part.

Katie had gotten used to public events over the years and even grew to like them. She used her social abilities to flutter around the room, making small talk with everyone. She walked over to Jessica, and the two stood together outside the door of the limo. Katie made eye contact with a few acquaintances in the crowd and gave them a smile and a small wave.

Hollywood was a small town, and she had gotten to know reporters and fans over the years. She knew how to play the game for Stephen.

Stephen emerged from the limo, and the crowd cheered. The flashes came more furiously. Reporters started yelling his name. He made his way over to Katie, and she took him by the arm.

He'd lost some of his looks over the years. Gone was his blonde surfer hair. It had turned grey long ago, and he left it natural. His tone and physique had softened over the years, but he was still recognizable as a once-buff young man. He hadn't let himself go, nor had he kept up with exercise over the years. He occupied an awkward middle ground.

Stephen waved to the crowd, and the roar grew. At that moment, Jake emerged from the limo, and the crowd's cheers reached a crescendo. Jessica flinched because the roar was so loud. Reporters began screaming all of their names in unison and Jessica found it difficult to know where to look.

The family traveled down the red carpet as a unit. Stephen and Katie went first, and Katie held onto Stephen's arm. Jake followed closely behind them, and Jessica brought up the rear.

As the approached a large movie poster, the group stopped and posed for pictures. This always made Jessica feel a little strange. She was 17, and her awkward teenage years had been captured on red carpets and in tabloids.

Jessica learned from her mother to put one leg at an angle and her hand on her hip. "It'll help you look your thinnest," she remembered her mother telling her. Also, their chin was down, so she didn't have a double chin in photos.

Jessica struck the pose in the line-up with her family. She noticed her mother doing virtually the same pose. It was easier for Jake and Stephen. They just had to stand there with their hands in their pockets, looking relaxed.

After the family photo, Jake, Stephen, and Katie walked over to the velvet rope, where reporters and cameramen were standing waiting to interview them. They each chose a different person, but many of the questions were the same.

Jessica continued down the red carpet a few feet and stood off to the side. She knew the reporters didn't want to talk to her.

"Are you proud of your son's first film?" a reporter asked Stephen.

"Yes, I couldn't be prouder of Jake," Stephen said, smiling. "He's been working very hard to follow in his father's footsteps. I also want to mention that I had nothing to do with his. He made it happen all on his own and that's one of the things that makes me so very proud of everything that he accomplished."

A few feet down the red carpet, Jake stood talking to another reporter.

"How does it feel to follow in your father's footsteps?"

"It's amazing," Jake said. "Ever since I was a little kid, I looked up to my father. I always knew that I wanted to be involved in the film business, and I was so excited to partner with his long-time producer-friend Gio Rossi on my first feature."

Katie was busy answering questions, too.

"You look amazing," a female reporter gushed to her. "How do you keep so fit?"

Katie smiled and laughed at her. "I think it's a combination of all-natural products and good genes. It also helps that I love to workout. We have a gym at home, and you'll find me working out there constantly."

"What are you working on next?" Another reporter asked Stephen.

"Well, I'm going to be producing another film with my long-time friend Leah Bennett. She's going to be starting as a hard New York City cop whose new partner may or may not be a serial killer," Stephen gushed.

"What are you working on next?" Another reporter asked the same question to Jake.

"I'm going to take my time and pick my next project," Jake said. "It's really important to me that I find material that I connect with. With this film, I felt a strong connection to the material. I was able to identify with the hurt that those parents must have been feeling to dump their baby in the desert. When I think about my next project, I want to make sure I have those same strong feelings toward the material in my next project. I'll know it when I see it."

"Your entire family is here tonight. How does that feel to all walk the red carpet together?" A reporter asked Katie.

"It's amazing. I love that Jessica is able to join us, too. It's her 18th birthday tomorrow, so we have a lot of important milestones this week."

"A lot has been made about your last name in the press over the years," another reporter chimed in, asking Katie. She turned slightly to face him and the camera next to him.

"Yes," she said and looked down slightly.

"The Dolls," the reporter said. "Stephen, Kate, Jake, and Jessica Doll."

Katie smiled.

The reporter continued, "It seems fitting that such a perfect family has a perfect last name."

"Yes," Katie gushed. "We are the perfect family."

PART II

9

November 8th, 2019

It wasn't a typical day in the Dollhouse. Usually, the house would be buzzing by 7 AM. Stephen would have been long out of the house and already settled into his office at the studio. He typically left the house around 6 AM and arrived at the office no later than 6:45 AM. He liked to be the first one in. It allowed him to get things done before the buzz of the day started.

He still occupied the same office on the studio lot that he had for the last 15 years. He directed film after film for the studio, but he began losing his passion for directing. Even while he was directing, it still felt like someone else was calling the shots. He wanted to be in charge of everything, so he transitioned to producing.

He loved having the final say. If he didn't like an actor, he would say no. If the director wanted more money to shoot and he felt it wasn't necessary, he would say no. If he didn't like the direction the script was heading, he'd fire the writer and hire a new one.

His reputation was earned by his ability to focus solely on the business. He was a man who knew what he wanted and wouldn't stop until he got it.

Stephen wasn't always this way. When he first met Katie, he was much less motivated. It was his experience on his first film, "Hard to Live," which made him this way. Even though the film was a hit, Stephen felt like a hired gun and was only there to be told what to do.

He fumbled his way through his second film and let the producers guide him. It really wasn't a strategic move; he just didn't know what he was doing. He allowed others to call the shots.

But, the key moment of hiring Leah Bennett to star in his third film was a major turning point. From that point on, he was calling the shots in his career.

Today was a rare day off for Stephen. Over the last almost twenty years, he has been constantly working. He was off on a location shoot, at his office interviewing writers, and on set making sure the director was getting the shots they needed. He worked 16-hour days, usually six days a week, and he never stopped.

With Jake's big premiere, he decided to take the day off. This was the first time his alarm was set later than 5:30 AM in years. He didn't want Katie waking him if his body would even allow him to sleep in.

When Jessica woke up for school, the house was quiet. She got up at 7:15 AM and showered.

Usually, when she emerged from her bedroom and headed to the kitchen, one of the housekeepers was already there making her mother's precious morning coffee. But this morning was different. Jessica wasn't sure if her mother had given the help the day off, but there was not a soul in sight.

Jessica rarely saw her mother in the mornings. Since she was 13, she had been getting up on her own and getting ready for school. Around that same time, her nanny, Stacey, left, and her mother decided she was getting too old for a nanny anyway.

It was a rough transition for Jessica. Stacey had been such a big part of her life since she was a baby; the first few months were tough without her. She left so abruptly that Jessica wasn't even able to mentally prepare.

Since then, Jessica had pretty much been on her own. Her mother, while loving her morning coffee, seemed to see the morning less and less over the years. On the weekends, Jessica would notice her getting out of bed at 11 AM or 12 PM and lumbering to the kitchen. She would stand there for an hour sipping coffee, which was the only time, day or night, that Jessica saw her mother eat or drink anything at all.

Jessica grabbed some fruit from the fridge and threw it into her backpack. She headed out the door.

Katie struggled to sleep at night. Last night was no different. The biggest difference was this morning, when she woke up, she'd be doing so next to Stephen. She grew so used to him being gone by the time she woke up; it was strange to have him there. She knew he wouldn't be happy if she woke him, so she did her best to be quiet.

It was also weird for her to be up so early. Since she had so much trouble sleeping at night, she would often stay in bed all morning. She would toss and turn all night in bed and finally fall asleep sometime after Stephen left. She would pull the covers over her head and drift off for as long as her body would allow it. She was usually back up and about by noon.

She had given the housekeepers the day off. She knew Stephen hated having so many people in the house during the day when he was around. She rarely had to worry about that anymore since he spent most days (and nights) in his office.

Katie made her way down to the kitchen. There was no coffee waiting for her. It had been a while since that had happened, too. One of the house staff was always around to ensure she had coffee whenever she wanted it.

She made her way to the Keurig machine in the far corner of the kitchen. She pulled out a drawer below it and pulled out a coffee pod. She slipped it in the machine, put a mug below the filter, and waited for the beautiful aroma to fill the air.

Within a few seconds, the machine hissed to life, and Katie had a steaming hot cup of coffee. Before the machine could even fully finish, she pulled the mug out and pressed it to her lips. The coffee burned her lips and mouth as she sipped, but she didn't care. She needed to feel the heat.

She stood and sipped and stared off into the pool in the backyard. Just beyond the pool, Katie could see the palm trees swaying in the breeze. Further along the horizon was the Pacific Ocean. It was one of the most beautiful views in all of Beverly Hills. Katie had seen it a million times. Even though her eyes were fixated on the view, her mind was somewhere else.

She felt her phone vibrate in her pocket. She pulled it out and looked at it. It was an alarm she had set. The time was 9 a.m. That meant Stephen's alarm would be going off upstairs, and he would be awake soon.

In a single motion, she slid the phone back into her pocket and turned to the door that led down into the basement.

Simultaneously, upstairs, Stephen slapped his alarm. He was surprised that he hadn't woken up before it, but he relished a few extra hours of rest.

He rolled over in the bed and found it empty. Katie was already up for the day. He briefly considered staying in bed a few more minutes, but he begrudgingly dragged himself out of bed and across the large bedroom to the bathroom.

He stepped inside and closed the door behind him. It was a large, classic-looking bathroom. To the left of him was a mirror nearly the entire length of the wall. There were double sinks, and Katie didn't allow anything to be left out on them. He kept all of his stuff in a hidden medicine cabinet behind the mirror.

Directly to Stephen's right was a small room containing the toilet. Just beside that was a large glass shower. The floor was tile, and the walls were marble with shiny gold fixtures. At the end of the bathroom was a large soaking tub that looked out through three large windows onto the backyard.

Stephen made his way to the shower, opened the glass door, and turned the hot water on as far as it would go. He waited for the steam to start rising and turned the cold water on ever so slightly. He dropped his shorts to the floor and stepped inside the steam shower.

As he stood under the scalding water, he thought of all the things he wanted to do during the day before he had to get ready for the premiere. It was a rare day off, but that didn't mean he was going to stop working.

He lathered up his hair, his one feature that hadn't changed much since his 20s, and let the hot water rinse the soap out.

Today was going to be a busy day for him. He quickly finished up his shower and dried off. He walked, wrapped only in his towel, out of the bathroom and into the bedroom. He heard his phone buzz on the nightstand. He adjusted course and sat on the side of the bed. He picked up his phone and looked at it. There was a motion alert from a camera in the basement.

He brought up the camera app. The motion was coming from the gym in the basement—at least, that was how the app still listed the camera. It hadn't been a gym in years. Katie used to use it to work out all the time, but when she finally stopped, she had the room converted into a lounge.

She brought in chairs and tables, purchased a hugely expensive piece of artwork, and had it hung. Stephen protested, but Katie persisted. Around this same time, she also drained the basement pool. The kids hadn't used it in years, and it sat next to this makeshift lounge, drying out and crumbling.

Katie set off the motion alert when she entered the lounge. Stephen didn't have motion alerts set for every room in the house, but he liked to keep tabs on Katie when she was in the lounge. He knew exactly why she went down there and what she was about to do.

Stephen watched on his phone as Katie stepped into the lounge. She looked around and turned on a lamp, which illuminated the room. She carried a coffee mug with her, and Stephen watched as she walked to the far side of the room, which held the largest credenza. It was at least 10 feet long and had nearly as many drawers.

Katie opened one of the bottom drawers and pushed aside some junk that was stored in it. Her back was to the camera, so Stephen couldn't see exactly what she was doing, but he didn't need to know the specifics.

He could see her pull something out of the drawer and place it on top of the credenza. As she bent back down to close the drawer, Stephen could see what it was. It was a tiny plastic bag filled with white pills and a small mirror.

Katie stood back up, blocking Stephen's view. He noticed her doing something, then bending over and bringing the mirror up to her nose. He didn't need to see anymore. He tossed his phone down on the bed and went over to his closet to get dressed.

He emerged fully clothed in a button-down shirt and jeans. He wore no socks and black slip-on loafers. He walked into the bathroom and slicked back his hair. This had been his signature look for years. Long blonde hair pushed back and a casual-but-not-too-casual outfit.

After he was finished, he grabbed his phone off of the bed and walked down the long hallway to the double staircase that led to the front door. He passed Jake's room. The door was still closed. He knew that meant that Jake was still sleeping in there.

He passed Jessica's room. The door was open, and her room was empty. She was already at school for the day. He passed a few more closed doors along the way. One was a bathroom. The others were former bedrooms that nannies had once occupied, which had been long vacant.

Stephen bounded down the stairs and found his keys on a small table just inside the front door. He pulled his phone out of his pocket and checked the camera app one more time. He saw Katie passed out in one of the large chairs in the lounge.

"Sleep it off," he said out loud to himself as he walked out of the front door.

She did sleep it off. Katie was sound asleep when a dream jolted her awake. She wasn't always able to sleep after she used but this time was different. She hadn't slept all night next to

Stephen. It wasn't uncommon. She could never relax when Stephen was around. He put her on edge. She always got her best sleep after he got up for work and left. She felt like then she could finally relax.

Stephen didn't get up at the crack of dawn today, which led to Katie tossing and turning all night and not being able to at least get a few hours of sleep when he left. So, instead, she got up, had a cup of strong black coffee like she always did, and slipped away to her hideaway to snort a line of Oxy.

Usually it gave her a bump of energy she needed to get through the day. Today, she was so exhausted that she passed out. She was dreaming vaguely of the sun. She couldn't remember exactly what her dream was about, but she remembered being really hot. She was panting in her sleep. It was one of these heavy breaths that shocked her out of her slumber.

She sat straight up in her chair and tried to focus. Her mind was hazy. She wasn't sure if it was from the bump or the lack of sleep. Her eyes focused on random objects around the room as she got her bearings. A shiny gold handle on one of the nearby tables. The swirly blue fabric of the chair across from her. The bright red nail polish began to chip off of her left pinky finger.

Finally, she came around enough to realize where she was. She had passed out on the lounge. She looked over at the credenza and saw her pills and mirror still lying there. She stood up quickly, too quickly, in fact, and had to steady herself on the chair. Once she had her balance, she walked over to the credenza, grabbed the mirror and pill bag, and shoved them back into the bottom drawer. She wiped a little powder off of the top of the credenza and walked back out of the room. She left all of the lights on.

She made her way up the stairs and emerged in the kitchen. She walked back over to the Keurig, grabbed a new mug, and made herself another cup of coffee. She was standing there sipping it when she noticed the clock on the wall. It was 10:59 AM. She took another sip of coffee as Jake entered the room.

"Morning, Mom," he said.

She was lost in her haze. It took her a few minutes to register that he was there, and she muttered, "Morning, baby."

She took another sip of the hot coffee. She knew it was hot. Her instincts told her that, but she was so numb from the pill that she wasn't even sure if it was burning her or not.

"Now, Mom," Jake said, walking over to stand next to her. "Don't forget that the limo is going to be here at 6 PM to pick us up."

She could hear the words as though they were coming from the next room. They were muffled in a way that she could only make out every other word. She heard forget. Limo. Pick up. She couldn't make sense of anything, so she took another sip of coffee to avoid having to think any longer.

"Mom," Jake said, a little louder this time. Katie looked up at him, and her glassy eyes met his.

He immediately knew what was happening. She had been in the basement again. He decided to speak again, slowly and clearly. "Don't forget, you need to be ready for the limo."

Katie realized what was happening. It was Jake. Her baby boy was standing next to her and reminding her of something. She couldn't quite remember what it was, but she hoped she could remember more as the pill wore off and her mind slowly returned.

She didn't want him to worry, so she did the motherliest thing she could think of at the moment. She put her hand to the side of his face and said, "I'll be ready."

He didn't believe her, but he knew he would be home in time to remind her again.

"Good. I need to run out and get a haircut and pick up my tux. I will be back around 3 PM. Jess should be home from school by then."

Katie pulled her hand down from his face and put it around the warmth of her mug.

"I'll text Dad to make sure he's home by then, too," Jake said.

Jake left his mother standing in the kitchen with her mug of coffee. He turned and walked the length of the house to the front door. He grabbed his keys off of the same table where Stephen kept his just as his phone buzzed from his pocket.

He pulled it out and looked at it. It was a text that read. "You need to come get your father NOW!"

It was from Leah Davis.

"Shit," Jake said to himself as he ran out the front door.

He hopped into his Mercedes SL 550, pushed the button that put the top down, and as soon as he could see the sky, he backed out of his parking spot and was on his way.

He knew exactly where he was going, and Leah didn't even need to tell him where they were. Luckily, it only took him 15 minutes to get there.

They were at Leah's house. She lived nearby in West Hollywood. When Jake pulled up outside her house, he found a familiar scene. His father's car was pulled up within inches of the front gate. The gate was closed, and he found his father pacing outside of it. This wasn't the first time this situation occurred, so Jake was sure he could take care of it.

Jake pulled his car off the street and parked directly behind Stephen's Range Rover.

"Dad," he said, getting out of the car and approaching Stephen.

"Forget it, Jake, just go home," Stephen snapped at him.

"Come on, let's go home. I want you to go with me."

"I'm not leaving here until she comes out and talks to me," Stephen yelled.

"I'm not coming out." Leah's voice could be heard from the intercom.

"Yes, you are, you bitch. You can't just do this to me."

"I can do anything I want," Leah's intercom said.

"I made you. I was the one who plucked you out of that audition and made you a star," Stephen seethed.

"Dad," Jake tried to say calmingly.

"That was 25 years ago, Stephen. You don't own me. You can't tell me I'm going to star in your next film. I don't want to do it," Leah said.

"You don't have a fucking choice. If you don't do it, I'm going to get the lawyers on you so fast."

"Go ahead and try. You forget that I've been in this business almost as long as you. I know people too, Stephen."

"What's the problem here, Dad?" Jake asked.

"This bitch thinks she's better than me now. She's going to star in my next film. I don't know why this is so hard for her to understand." Stephen continued to pace back and forth in front of the gate.

"Leah?" Jake asked. He always found himself in the position of being a peacemaker.

"He wants to shoot it in New York City. I told him no. I can't leave here for four months to do that. I have obligations here, and I'm not going to do it."

"You bitch," Stephen yelled again.

"Dad," Jake said, raising his voice. "Calm down."

"Don't you tell me to calm down." Stephen turned his rage toward his son. His face was red and flush. He had a hard time being told no. Once he was told no, his temper flared, and he had little control over it.

Before he could respond, Jake noticed a motorcycle pull up and stop a few houses down. The driver took his helmet off and was going through his backpack. Jake knew he was a paparazzi.

"Dad, look," Stephen said, gesturing his eyes down the street toward the motorcyclist. "Let's not cause a scene here, or it's going to be online in minutes."

Stephen knew Jake was right. He took a deep breath and walked over to the intercom. He said quietly into it, "This isn't over bitch. I'll be back."

Jake rolled his eyes as Stephen hopped into his Range Rover.

"I'm sorry, Leah," he yelled in the direction of the intercom.

There was no response.

Inside, Leah closed out the intercom app on her phone and put it down on the coffee table. She let out a big sigh.

"You know what he's like," a voice said from the couch next to her. It was Jessica.

"Yes," Leah said. "It's been 25 years; I'm used to his tricks and manipulations by now."

"How could you put up with that for so long?" Jessica asked her.

"You can get used to anything in this town," Leah said.

Jessica knew exactly what she was talking about. She wasn't even out of high school yet, but she knew her family was anything but normal.

"Yes, I know what you mean," Jessica mumbled.

Leah looked concerned. Suddenly, all thoughts of Stephen drained from her head, and she was laser-focused on Jessica.

"What's bothering you?" Leah asked with genuine concern. It always caught Jessica off guard when someone showed genuine concern for her.

"Oh," Jessica said, looking down. "It's just the usual."

"Well, I know how big of a pain in the ass your dad can be. What about your mom? How are things with Katie?" Leah turned to face Jessica.

"The usual," Jessica said. "She focuses what little attention she can muster on Jake. She's not terrible to me or anything. I try to focus on understanding I could have it much worse."

"You shouldn't have to think like that. You deserve to have a family who loves you." Leah was sincere.

"I know. That's one of the reasons I really love that you let me come here on those days when I just can't face school."

"You know this is always a safe place for you," Leah said. "Any time you need me, I'm going to be here for you."

Jessica's phone buzzed. She looked down and saw a text message from Katie.

"Speak of the devil," Jessica said. "I've got to go."

***

Jessica walked up a concrete staircase to the second floor. She walked down an outdoor hallway with a rusty iron railing to her left and a chipped white wall to her right. The sun beat down directly on her, making her uncomfortably hot.

Every so often, she passed a teal blue door on the white wall, marked with rusty iron numbers. She passed 11, then 12. Then she pulled her phone out of her pocket and opened her texts.

She first saw the text from her mother. "Can you get me another bump after school?" It read. It wasn't the first time that her mother asked her to get drugs. It was becoming increasingly common. Jessica wasn't quite sure where her mother was getting them before, but her well must have run dry as every few days Katie was asking her for more. Luckily, in the halls of her high school, nearly every one of her classmates had some kind of hookup, so it wasn't difficult to find.

Jessica scrolled to the next text. It was from a Los Angeles number, but Jessica didn't have the contact's name saved in her phone. The text read, "I'm in room 13."

By the time she looked up from her phone, she was in front of the teal door with a rusty 13 on it. She considered knocking, but she reached back down to her phone and texted back, "I'm here."

She stepped back from the door to give herself some space and was nearly against the iron rail. It was much hotter in the valley than when she left home. She lifted her forearm and wiped the sweat from her brow.

She vaguely heard movement from inside the room as the teal door swung open and revealed a man. He was at least five years older than Jessica. He was thin and wore a white tank top. He had sleeves of tattoos down both arms. Jessica had trouble making out much detail since they were so dense. They stopped at his shoulders and were hidden behind his tank top. Jessica could see through the white of the shirt that his chest was tattooed as well.

He had long brown hair pulled back haphazardly into a man bun. He wore a chain around his neck. His soft features betrayed the rest of his tough-man look.

"Hi Jessica," he said.

He stood and looked at her for a minute. "Hi, Mason," she replied.

"Come in," he said. He stepped aside as Jessica noticed his dark brown eyes for the first time. She stepped inside the room and noticed it was much cooler inside than outside in the heat. She was thankful for that.

She passed a small bathroom on her right and walked to the main part of the room. It was sparsely decorated. There was a double-sized bed, a table with a lamp, and a small couch where another man sat.

This man was similar in age to Mason. He looked much different. This man was muscular and tan. He wore a black T-shirt that was too tight. It looked like his biceps might split the shirt at any minute. He wore a backward white baseball cap. His features were dark, but his eyes were lighter than Mason's. He had a full beard that was neatly trimmed and long blonde hair that was slicked back.

His arms were tattooed on his sleeves. Jessica couldn't make out much detail in any of them without staring for too long, but it was obvious that the man had spent many hours having them done. Some of the tattoos peeked out from his shirt collar, almost climbing up his neck.

"This is Harrison," Mason said, introducing them.

Jessica was uncomfortable with his presence. Something was familiar about him, but he felt foreign at the same time.

"Hey," she blurted in his direction, avoiding eye contact.

"Have a seat," Mason said to her.

Jessica sat on the corner of the bed. She still avoided eye contact with Harrison, but she could tell he was looking right at her.

"Oh, this might help," Mason said. He crossed between Harrison and Jessica and grabbed something off of the table. He held up a lighter and a small bag of pot. "How about I light up some of this to take the edge off."

"Sure," Jessica said. "I can't have too much. I have to be lucid for my brother's premiere tonight."

Mason let out a chuckle. He kneeled near the table and began to roll a joint.

"Won't your parents wonder why you came home from school stoned?" Harrison asked.

"I don't think my parents would even notice if I didn't come home from school most days," Jessica responded. She still didn't look at him.

"Sorry, you're the poor little rich girl, right?" Harrison snapped.

"Look, I don't have to stay here right now. I can walk right out the door." Jessica responded with anger.

"Woah, woah, woah," Mason tried to smooth the tension. "It's fine. We're going to light this thing up, and everything is going to be ok."

Jessica wasn't sure if anything was going to ease the tension in the room. Mason finished rolling the joint and handed it to her. She grabbed the lighter from off the table and lit up the joint. She inhaled deeply and took all of the smoke into her lungs. She held her breath as long as he could and calmly exhaled the smoke.

She felt a quick calming effect. She passed the joint to Harrison, who did the same. He passed it back to Mason.

Before Mason took a long puff, he said, "See, now, doesn't that feel better?"

Jessica was starting to relax. She looked Harrison in the eyes for the first time and could tell he was relaxing, too.

She took another deep breath and let go of her anxiety.

10

November 9th, 2019

"Dinner is ready," Jessica heard her mom's voice as an announcement on the Amazon Echo on her desk. Since the house was so big, and Jessica tried to avoid as much face-to-face interaction with her parents as she could, they would often use the Echoes to communicate with each other. It wasn't uncommon to hear someone's voice asking a question and then another answering it. Like cameras, there was one in virtually every room of the house.

Jessica sighed and left her room, heading toward the dining room. She had made no special efforts to get dressed up, even though she knew her mother would be and expected them all to be.

This was part of her mother's idea of perfection. They would all get dressed up on their birthdays and have dinner together precisely at 7 PM. Jessica wasn't exactly sure how this tradition began, but it happened as long as she could remember. She wasn't even sure why they had to continue this, but it didn't matter whose birthday it was; her mother always made them do this.

As Jessica approached the dining room, she could hear voices. She knew the housekeepers had already prepared the meal. There was no way her mother was going to cook it. She would just present it in its most perfect form. Her mother was good at that — not the behind-the-scenes part but presenting perfection.

Jessica rounded the corner into the dining room, and she saw everything set out perfectly. The table had large candelabras set in the middle of the table with long white wax candles with flames burning high. There were exactly four place settings around the too-large table. They each had the best china and perfect silverware. Cloth napkins and named place cards. The food was laid out on platters around the table. Even with the excessive amount of food that was prepared, it still came nowhere close to filling the table.

Her mother, father, and brother were already sitting around the table. As she knew they would be, the entire family was dressed up. Her mother had one of her trademark form-fitting, flowing gowns on. This one was bright red and highlighted exactly how skinny her mother was. Her father wore a standard black tuxedo, and Jake was dressed to match.

"Oh my god," Katie said. "You are absolutely not going to be sitting here with us looking like that."

Jessica was wearing jeans and a black sweatshirt. This was Jessica's go-to outfit, even when the Los Angeles weather dictated that it was too hot.

"Mom, it's fine. It's my birthday," Jessica pleaded.

"Absolutely not." Katie was firm.

"Maybe you could just put on something a little nicer?" Jake said. Jessica didn't take it as an attack. Her brother had settled into the role of peacekeeper in the family. Most times, she appreciated it. She had grown closer to her brother as she grew older. He was the closest thing she had to someone to count on.

"No," Katie said, unwilling to bend. "This is your birthday dinner. You know the dress code." Jessica noticed as she talked that she had a small crystal glass of scotch in her hand. Katie's typical drinks were coffee in the morning and scotch anytime past noon.

Jessica relented. "Happy birthday to me, I guess."

"Go back upstairs. The housekeeper just brought several of your dresses back from the cleaners. I don't care which one, but go get changed now."

Katie took a large sip of her scotch, and Jessica left the room to head back upstairs.

"You don't have to be so hard on her mom," Jake said.

Katie set her glass down on the table and pulled out her chair. She was obviously her usual drunk and high combination, and she struggled with her balance as she tried to sit down in her chair.

Jake was about to jump up and help her when she finally managed. She sat with her back to the entrance to the room. Clockwise from her was Stephen. He had remained quiet throughout this interaction. He was face-down on his phone the entire time.

Jake sat across from his mother. The empty seat to his left was for his sister. These were their assigned seats for the birthday dinners. Jake couldn't remember another time that his entire family gathered around this table other than for birthday dinners.

"She needs to learn how to be a part of this family. She's always marching to the beat of her own drum," Katie said.

Stephen lifted his head from his phone. "Why don't you just have another drink to calm your nerves?"

"What is that crack supposed to mean?" Katie seethed.

"Hey," Jake interjected. "This is your idea, Mom. You're the one who insists that we have these birthday dinners for each other. The very least the two of you can do tonight is behave."

"It's never me you have to worry about," Stephen said.

"Of course not, Stephen." Katie stared directly at him. "Everything you've done in your life is perfect and beyond reproach."

"How would you even know what I've done with my life? You're barely with it enough to know what's going on with your own life."

"Oh?" Katie asked. "I know enough to take down that life of yours at any point."

"Enough," Jake interjected again, loudly this time. "If you two don't stop it now, we're going to call an end to this—"

Jake was cut off as the entire room went black. The lights that had been illuminating the room were suddenly gone. The cool air that was being pumped through the vents to keep the house cool on this unusually warm November evening abruptly stopped. The loud pop of an appliance stopping could be heard from the other room.

Stephen, Katie, and Jake were left sitting around the table, lit only by the candles that were supposed to be providing ambiance.

"Oh shit," Stephen said. "This is all we need tonight."

"Do you think it's just us, or is the entire neighborhood out?"

Jake pulled out his phone and turned on the flashlight. "I'll go look."

He used the light to illuminate a path from the dining room into the kitchen. From there, he could look out through the walls of windows and out onto the back terrace. He could see the moonlight glistening off of the pool. Beyond the edge of the pool, he had a view of neighboring houses before seeing the ocean. All of the other houses glowed in the warm November sky.

"It's just us," he yelled back to his parents.

"Why isn't the generator kicking on?" He heard his father yell back from the other room.

Stephen appeared in the doorway, also using his phone as a flashlight. Jake noticed this just before yelling back at him.

"I don't know. It usually only takes a few seconds, right?"

"Yes," Stephen replied.

They stood in silence for a few more moments to see if anything would change. It didn't. Jake noticed how eerily quiet the house was. There was almost always some sort of unnoticed background noise happening. The air conditioner blows air from the vents. An unknown appliance humming. But there was nothing. It brought a shiver to his spine, but he shook it off.

"Go check it out," Stephen said.

Jake rolled his eyes, but luckily, his father couldn't see in the dark.

"Fine, fine. I'll be right back," he said.

Jake shined his flashlight down on the floor and walked over to the basement door. He pulled the door open and stopped.

He never much liked the basement. It always felt cold and a place that only the adults went. He had memories from when he was a child of his father spending evenings down in the screening room watching old movies. Jake would sometimes venture down and try to sit with his father, but the movies never really interested him. He would get bored and run back to his room to play with his toys.

Those days ended years ago. Now, the only person who came down here was his mother. He knew exactly why she was going down there.

It always felt like there were secrets locked in the basement, and by opening that door, he was going to expose all of their secrets.

He shook it off. That was silly. His family was his family. They didn't hold any secrets from each other. Sure, there were plenty of things Jake knew about that they never spoke about, but they weren't secrets. The basement was just a room like any other room in the house. There were no secrets to be let out by just opening the door.

He took his first step down the staircase and then another. It was fine. Nothing was changing. By the time he made it down to the third step, he could smell chlorine. The pool downstairs had been drained many years before, but the smell of chlorine never fully went away.

Jake continued down the staircase until he made it to the bottom. He turned and walked into the screening room. He used his phone to light the way, but the basement was even darker than upstairs. At least upstairs, there was some candlelight, and the kitchen had a soft blue glow from the moonlight coming in. The basement was completely pitch black. Nothing was going to penetrate the basement. No light. No fresh air.

Jake shined his light around, trying to get a full look at the screening room. He hadn't been in there for years. The old black leather recliners were still in the same place. They look dusty, some rotting, from years of being exposed to the chlorine from the pool, just a few rooms over.

He noticed some water damage at the top of one of the walls. Compared to other areas of the house, the room had certainly fallen into disrepair.

His mother kept the main floors beautiful, but this felt like what was underneath had just been forgotten.

Jake reached the door on the far side of the screening room. This door led to the storage area where they kept old junk. This room also housed all of the mechanical equipment that kept the house running. The furnace, the pool equipment, the fuse box, the generator, and more things Jake didn't even know what they were. They were all housed in this room.

He swung the door open and was hit in the face with a breath of hot air. The air conditioning was certainly not working in this room. He coughed as he tried to exhale some of the hot, stale air.

He held his hand out in front of him, and the flashlight on his phone illuminated the room. The light bounced off of the polished concrete floors. He noticed rack after rack of boxes. Some are in large plastic tubs, and others are just sitting on shelves. Some had writing on the sides detailing contents. Christmas decorations, pool supplies, or gym equipment were common themes. Others were blurs and revealed no hints of what was inside.

Jake took his time walking slowly down the long aisle of boxes. They were stacked from the floor to the ceiling. They made it seem as if the room was one long hallway. In reality, it was a square-shaped room, but Jake needed to go down the hallway of boxes to get to the generator on the other side of the room.

He shined his light back and forth on boxes, trying to stay in the middle of the aisle as he walked. He felt something hit his foot and heard it slide across the floor.

"Shit," he said out loud. At that same moment, there was a loud bang behind him. He jerked around and shined his light in the direction from which he had just walked. He saw the door leading out to the screening room had slammed shut.

"Hello?" he asked no one in particular.

He suddenly felt very silly. This wasn't a horror movie, he thought. There's no one stalking you in your Beverly Hills basement. No one could even stand a chance at hopping the gate or the large wall that surrounded the property. The door was probably on a hinge to keep it shut, and it just closed itself.

Jake took a deep breath and turned around. He shined his flashlight further down the aisle and took a few more steps. The object that he kicked was lying ahead a few feet. His light didn't shine quite far enough for him to make it out clearly. He took a few more steps, and the light glared off of the object.

He took a few more steps, and it came into clear view. It was a picture frame. Jake stood nearly on top of it and shined his light down on it.

The frame itself was shattered from Jake kicking it. Shards of glass stuck out everywhere. Jake carefully picked it up, and several shards of glass fell back to the floor, echoing throughout the room.

He looked at the photo in the frame. It was of his parents from when they were about his age. His father had his arm around his mother, and they were both smiling. They looked so happy. It was a stark contrast to the scene he had just witnessed upstairs.

Jake managed to crack a smile. It brought back memories of happier days when he was younger. He wasn't sure if everything was happy back then or if his memory was whitewashing it, but it was certainly much different than his life now.

Jake shined the light at a different angle to get a better view of the photo. His smile quickly faded this time.

A shard of glass from the frame had pierced the photo. From the angle in which Jake was holding it, it looked like the shard of glass went straight into his father's neck.

Jake shuddered and dropped the frame back down to the floor.

***

Jessica was nearly in her room when the power went out. Just as she grabbed for the doorknob to open the door to her bedroom, the entire hallway went dark. There was absolutely no light in the hallway. There were no windows or open doors. Jessica smacked the back of her hand on the doorknob and let out a yelp.

"Ouch," she said to herself.

She tried again, this time grabbing the doorknob. She threw open the door to her room, and it smacked off of the wall. Her room was very dark but not as bad as the hallway. Some light from outside was shining through her window.

She reached into her pocket and pulled out her phone. She turned on the flashlight and shined it around her room. Through the darkness, she found her bed and made her way over to it.

She was dreading getting dressed and going back downstairs. She plopped down on the bed and let her arms hang and shoulders droop. She looked down at her phone, turned off the flashlight, and fell backward onto her bed with her arms straight out. Her phone fell from her hand and landed on the bed just a few inches away.

Jessica looked at the ceiling. She could see a vague swirling pattern as the lights from outside danced on the white ceiling.

She tried to zone out, forgetting it was her birthday and that her family was waiting for her downstairs. However, she could not forget or get thoughts of them out of her head.

Jessica had some level of awareness of the privilege she had in life. She knew that her family was wealthy. She knew that her father was a powerful producer in Hollywood. She knew that he'd always pressured her brother to follow in his footsteps. She tried not to take any of that for granted.

Still, she yearned for more in her family life. While dysfunctional, Jake seemed to enjoy a different type of relationship with their parents. The only time Jessica had ever seen her mother's eyes spark to life was when she was looking at

Jake. Jessica was never afforded that same type of relationship with her mother.

She wasn't sure what created it, but there was always a distance between her and her mother. Maybe it was the fact that she was primarily raised by her nanny, or maybe it was the fact that Jake was the firstborn or the boy. Jessica wasn't quite sure.

She didn't blame Jake for any of it. He had always been there for her growing up. Jake always looked out for her, and she appreciated it. If she ever needed anything, she knew she could turn to Jake, and she appreciated it.

If there was a distance between her and her mother, there was a canyon between her and her father. They really didn't interact other than superficial pleasantries. He provided for the family, but he worked so much that they never had the time required to create a relationship. He would be around here and there, and that was the best she could hope from him.

She was grateful, though, that he didn't put the same kind of pressure on her that he put on Jake. With Jake, it seemed like his father had a one-track mind. Jake was going to go into show business, and it was settled. There was no negotiating. Jake seemed to handle the pressure well, but Jessica always wondered what it was like to constantly be under pressure from their father.

All of these thoughts were swirling in Jessica's head as her eyes adjusted to the darkness. Soon, the swirling lights on the ceiling came into better focus. She was able to tell it was clouds moving across the moon. It was the soft glow of lights coming from Beverly Hills.

A large shadow moved across the room. It went quickly from left to right. Jessica got a chill down her spine. This wasn't a cloud or a car outside. This was something more immediate and menacing. Someone was in the room with her.

She sat up straight.

"Hello," she asked into the darkness.

There was no response.

She reached down for her phone. She couldn't find it. She patted her arms around the bed again. It was gone. Someone had taken it.

Should she go for the door? Try to hide under the bed? Stay still? Had she made the entire thing up?

She sat frozen for a few moments, racing thoughts through her head. But nothing happened. Maybe she had made the entire thing up, and she was just afraid of being in the dark.

There's no one there, she thought. She relaxed her shoulders a bit. She allowed herself to exhale.

Suddenly, Jessica felt a cold hand wrap around her mouth. She felt another firmly grip her shoulder.

"Shhhh," a gravelly voice spilled from the darkness. "Don't say anything."

***

"What is taking Jake so long?" Katie asked. She was still sitting at the table, illuminated by candlelight, drinking her scotch.

Stephen stood on the other side of the table from her, pacing back and forth.

"It's only been a couple of minutes," Stephen said. "Would you just calm down?"

"I feel like you've been saying that to me every day for years now, Stephen," she said, slamming her glass down on the table.

The noise startled him, and he turned to face her.

"You've always been so high-strung," he said to her.

"High-strung?" She asked.

"Yes, you put on this show like you're charming and have everything put together, but underneath it all, you're really just a lost girl from the Midwest."

"Oh, should we talk about who we really are?" Katie asked. "You put on this show that you're this powerful producer, but you're still that same aimless boy from Orange County who would be nothing without me."

Stephen scoffed. "I do my job every single day without you. I think I've learned a thing or two along the way."

"Yes, and I was the one behind the scenes that was pushing you along the way the entire time."

"You're giving yourself too much credit." Stephen laughed. "As usual."

"And who would you give the credit to?" Katie asked.

"I'm going to take the credit. I'm good at my job, and that's why I've been so successful."

"Oh, that's great!" Katie exclaimed. She stood up and walked over to him. She looked him right in the eye. With her heels on, she was nearly as tall as him. "Do you know why we always talk to each other this way?"

"What way?" Stephen asked. He knew exactly what she was talking about, but he took a small amount of pleasure in making everything more difficult for her.

"You know exactly what I'm talking about. We can't even have a conversation with each other for two minutes anymore, Stephen."

"I suppose that's my fault, too, right?" He laughed at her.

"It's both of our faults. But the problem lies in you."

"Oh, yeah?" He laughed again. "And you know what my problems are?"

"I sure do, Stephen." She seethed with anger. "I know you better than anyone else. That's the problem. I'm not one of your yes-men. You've surrounded yourself with people that will bow down to you and tell you that every shitty idea you ever had is perfect."

"I have a lot of great ideas," Stephen said. He believed it in his own mind.

"I'm not one of those yes men. And you can't take it when I call you on your bull shit."

"Do we have to rehash this again right now?" Stephen asked.

A loud crash came from the kitchen.

Katie jumped and grabbed Stephen's arm. He looked down and shook her off.

"What was that?" She asked, grabbing his arm again.

"I don't know. Something fell over from the sounds of it."

"Maybe it was Jake bumping into something on his way back?" She whispered.

"Jake?" Stephen yelled toward the kitchen. There was no response. "Let's go find out."

Stephen took a step toward the kitchen. Katie followed him closely.

They walked together in unison, taking small steps. The entire house was silent. Whatever the loud crash they heard wasn't happening again. With each step Stephen took, Katie was right behind him. They were no longer used to being this physically close together.

Stephen took a few more steps, and they crossed through the doorway that led into the kitchen.

The kitchen looked much darker at first. Their eyes needed to adjust. The dining room was still being lit by the candles.

Blue moonlight shined through the wall of windows in the kitchen. It almost crossed Katie's mind that the room looked so peaceful, but before she could finish the thought, her heart began to pound. It beat faster and faster the more steps they took into the kitchen.

"Do you have your phone? Use the flashlight?" Katie asked.

"It's back on the dining room table," Stephen said.

She rolled her eyes, but he couldn't see in the dark. She remain clutched to his side.

136

They walked to the middle of the kitchen and stopped. Stephen squinted as he tried to look around, and Katie attempted to do the same. As their eyes adjusted to the darker room, they both focused on different things.

Katie looked at the island in the middle of the kitchen. She could barely make out the coffee maker behind it. She focused on the spot where she spent so much time standing and sipping her coffee.

Stephen looked around the room further. He noticed that the door on the far side of the room that led to the basement was open.

"Jake?" He yelled in the general direction of the door.

There was no response.

Stephen felt Katie's fingers dig into his arm.

"Hey," he yelped. As he was turning to face her, he noticed something outside on the patio. He saw that Katie was staring right at it.

It took him a minute to register what he was looking at. It was a person.

There was a person on the patio staring directly through the glass, looking at them. He couldn't see the person's face. He couldn't tell if it was a man or a woman. The figure was dressed all in black. Long black pants. Long black sleeves. Surely too hot for the warm weather, Stephen briefly thought.

The person's face was covered except for a white, featureless mask. The person had a black hood pulled up to the edges of the mask. They held one hand down by their side. They appeared to be holding something in their hand, but

Stephen couldn't make it out. The person raised their other hand and waved at Stephen and Katie through the glass. Katie gripped Stephen's arm even harder.

Stephen could make out what the figure was holding. It was a brick. They raised their hand above their heads and, in a swift motion, threw the brick at the glass.

Katie screamed as the glass shattered and gave the person entry into the house.

11

November 9th, 2019

Jake heard the crashing coming from upstairs. Even with the size of the house, there was no mistaking the sound of breaking glass. This wasn't the sound of someone dropping a coffee mug, this sounded like a door or a window shattering.

He turned around and quickly made his way back down the aisle of boxes to the door. He grabbed at the handle. The door was locked. He shined the flashlight on his phone down at the knob. There was no way to unlock it from the inside. It required a key that Jake didn't have.

Jake tried the knob again. It wouldn't budge. Jake was interrupted when he heard movement behind him. He turned around quickly and was able to make out through the shelves of boxes a stream of light coming from the exterior door on the other side of the room.

The door led out the side of the house with a path around to the back patio and pool area.

Someone had opened the door. Moonlight and the soft glow of Beverly Hills shone through the open space. It wasn't enough to light up the room, but just enough to illuminate a few feet in front of the door.

Jake quickly switched off the flashlight on his phone and quietly made his way back over to the racks of boxes. He peered through an open space on one of the shelves and noticed a figure appear in the doorway.

Jake could only see the outline of the person. They appeared to be dressed all in black with a hood and some kind of mask. Jake couldn't make out any features on the mask, but it appeared to be a cheap Halloween mask.

The figure walked from the doorway into the room. Jake was afraid he would lose track of the person, but the figure quickly turned on a flashlight. Immediately, light filled the room. Jake was afraid of being seen, so he ducked down to the ground.

If the figure were trying to get in the house, he would have to go right past Jake. The only way from one side of the room, without navigating through a sea of junk that had been accumulating for years, was to take the clear aisle that Jake was standing in.

The figure was doing just that. Jake noticed that the light shined directly toward the aisle, and the figure moved toward it with purpose.

Jake tried to adjust his eyes to the darkness. He needed to find a place to hide, or the figure was going to run right into him. He willed his eyes to see better, but it was no use. The bright

140

light of both his and the figure's flashlight had made his pupils grow wide and unwilling to adjust.

He started to quickly feel around on the bottom shelves. Most of them held boxes that were two or three feet tall. If he could just find an empty spot, he could squeeze into it. He carefully felt a box. He didn't want to knock anything over and give away his location. He wasn't even sure that the intruder had seen him, so there was a chance he could not be spotted if he could get onto a shelf.

He felt another box and began to move quickly down the aisle toward the exterior door. The intruder's light got brighter and brighter as the figure got closer to the other end of the aisle.

If Jake didn't find a spot before the intruder got to the other end of the aisle, he'd be a sitting duck. He moved quicker, remaining crouched down to the ground. Another box. Then another box. There were no empty spaces.

The light grew brighter. Jake knew he only had seconds. Another box. Then, just beyond that box, Jake caught a break. There was an empty space on the bottom shelf. He didn't wait to find out how large it was. He threw himself into the space, banging his head off of a shelf on the way in. The shelf vibrated just as the figure rounded the corner and shined his light down the aisle.

Jake quickly pulled his legs in and wedged himself behind a box.

The intruder quickly made his way down the aisle. He walked with purpose toward the interior door. Jake bravely peeked out from behind the box as the intruder passed, allowing him to get a better look at him.

By his stature and walk, he was obviously a male. He was at least six feet tall. Jake estimated a little more. He wore all black and a black hood. Jake was right about his mask. It was some sort of cheap children's Halloween mask. It was an innocent-looking cat. The cat had a pink nose and whiskers coming out of it. It had a giant grin on its face exposing a mouth overstuffed with white teeth.

The man had cut the eye holes out on the mask to be larger. Jake was slightly creeped out by it. Since he only caught a glimpse of the man, he couldn't see his eyes clearly. The mask barely covered his face, as it was obviously meant for a child.

The intruder passed Jake and approached the interior door. He grabbed the knob, and it was locked. Jake could barely see him from this angle behind the box. He moved his arm to see if he could get a better view, and it smacked into the side of the box. The entire shelf vibrated again.

The Cat Mask man quickly turned around and shined his flashlight back down the aisle. Jake remained perfectly still. He didn't even notice that he was holding his breath. Cat Mask took a few steps back down the aisle toward Jake. He shined his light left, then right on the shelves of boxes that lined the aisle.

He slowly looked around, took a few more steps, and stood directly in front of Jake. Jake slowly pulled himself into a ball behind the large box so that he was hidden as much as possible.

The man shined his flashlight up and down the shelf. Jake held his breath again. He pulled his hand into a fist and mentally prepared himself for a fight if the man tried to pull him out from behind the box. He hoped the man didn't have a weapon.

From Jake's perspective, he could only see light around the edges of the box behind him. He had to guess from how bright the light was where the man was shining the light. The brighter the light got, the more Jake squinted. He was sure he was going to be found.

But the opposite happened. The light went from bright to dim. Jake heard the man's footsteps move away from him. Jake mustered up the courage to again look out from behind the box.

He saw the man again approach the interior door. The man tried the knob again. He had the same issue as Jake. The door was locked. Jake watched as Cat Mask pushed his hand into his pocket and pulled out a small shiny object. It was a key.

Cat Mask placed the key in the doorknob and turned. The door popped open, and the man disappeared into the house.

Jake was confused. Who was this man, and where did he get a key to their house?

**

Katie's reflexes had never been so quick. As soon as she saw the brick in the man's hand, she screamed and let go of Stephen's arm. She turned around and ran toward the front door. She didn't actually see the brick crashing through the window since she was already facing the other direction, but there was no doubt that's what the loud crash was.

Stephen wasn't quite so quick. He stood and watched as the glass came crashing into the house. Shards covered the kitchen floor. He saw the moonlight reflect a thousand times as the glass door crumbled.

When his mind finally registered what was going on, he also turned and ran. He was about two steps behind Katie. They ran across the kitchen and toward the foyer, where the two staircases led upstairs.

Stephen caught up to Katie pretty quickly. She was trying to run in heels and was trying her hardest not to slip on her dress or the slippery marble floor. Stephen grabbed her by the arm.

Her step turned into a slide, but she didn't lose her balance. She couldn't tell if he was trying to help steady her or pushing her out of the way to get an advantage.

"Go! Go!" He screamed at her. She assumed he was trying to help.

Stephen reached the front door first. Katie slammed into it just a second after he reached it. Stephen reached down and tried the knob. It was locked. He fumbled with the locks on the door.

"Hurry, Stephen!" Katie screamed at him. Then she turned around to see where the man in the mask was.

He was coming up quickly behind them. Katie was stunned, looking at his mask. She got a better look at it than she had through the glass. It was white and featureless, but it looked like someone had cut the eye holes out to be two sizes too large. The white mask reminded Katie of wax. Almost as if someone had taken their face and dipped it in hot wax so many times that all of the features had disappeared and only left the general outline of a face.

Katie heard Stephen still fumbling with the locks beside her. She noticed that the man in the wax mask was no longer holding a brick in his hand. He held something else. Katie fixated on it. It was hard to see in the dark, but Katie got a clear glimpse of it when the light from the man's flashlight bounced off of it. It was a large, shiny silver knife.

Wax Mask ran straight toward them and raised the knife above his head.

"Stephen," Katie cried. "Look out!"

The man was within a foot of them with the knife raised above his head. He took another step and brought the knife straight down in a stabbing motion. Luckily, Stephen had heard Katie's cry, and he was mid-duck when the knife slashed passed his head, and the tip wedged itself in the wood of the front door.

Stephen pushed Katie away from the door. Wax Mask struggled with the knife, which was firmly wedged in the front door. He tried to pull it out, but the hardwood held it firm. He began to wiggle it from side to side to remove it from the door.

Katie nearly tumbled over when Stephen pushed her away from the door. She stumbled, and her heel nearly gave out from under her. She regained her balance just as Stephen grabbed her hand and pulled her toward the left staircase.

Stephen nearly pulled Katie's arm out of the socket, trying to get her to run up the stairs. She tried her best to keep up, but the back of her dress kept getting caught on her shoes. The waist of her dress was also snug and limited movement.

Katie hurried up the stairs, partially being propelled by Stephen's pulling. She finally regained her balance just as Stephen stopped moving, and she slammed into the back of him. She was able to balance herself by gripping tighter to his hand.

It took Katie a moment to realize why Stephen had stopped. Directly across from them on the right-hand staircase was Wax Mask. He was standing on the same step as them on the opposite staircase. If they both continued, they would meet at the platform on top of the stairs.

The moonlight coming in the windows above the door illuminated the staircases in a bright blue light. The front of the house didn't have the same glow from the hills of Beverly Hills as the back of the house, and this eerie blue light made Wax Mask's mask even colder looking.

"What do you want?" Stephen asked. There was no response.

"Who are you? Do you want money?" Katie tried. There was still no response.

Wax Mask was having fun with them. He took the knife that he was able to pry out of the door. He held it in his right hand, held it horizontally by the blade, and pointed it right at the two of them.

A chill cut through Katie. She imagined what the knife would feel like cutting into her flesh. He didn't want money. He wanted to harm them.

Stephen looked at the top of the staircase. He surveyed their options. They were safe for a few minutes. Wax Mask couldn't get them, but at some point, they were going to have to make a move.

"Jake," Katie screamed. "Get out of the house."

Stephen looked over at Wax Mask. He was perched, waiting for them to make a move. No matter which direction Stephen ran, he knew the man would catch up to them.

"Jessica," Katie screamed again. "Run! Get out!"

Stephen leaned over and whispered into Katie's ear. "Go upstairs and get Jessica."

Before she could totally comprehend what he had whispered, Stephen let go of her hand and darted down the stairs. Katie realized what he meant, and she ran up the stairs.

When she reached the top of the stairs, she looked across to make sure Wax Mask hadn't run up his staircase after her. She didn't see him. She looked down, and she saw Stephen standing at the bottom of the left staircase and Wax Mask standing at the bottom of the right staircase. There were about eight feet separating the men, and they were standing there looking directly at each other. Katie briefly wondered who was going to flinch and move first.

But neither man did. They both just stood there, breathing heavily and staring. The staring contest was ended by an unexpected entry. Katie watched as another man wearing a Cat Mask ran out from the back of the house and stopped right between the two men. Cat Mask looked over at Wax Mask, and they both turned to Stephen.

Katie knew what they were thinking. She had to do something.

"Hey, assholes! Up here," she yelled at the top of her lungs.

It worked. Wax Mask turned, looked at her, and ran up the right staircase toward her. She had a good head start on him. She ran from the platform to the hallway that would take her toward the bedrooms and deeper into the house. She didn't need to look behind her to know that Wax Mask was following her. She could feel him.

She entered the hallway and was shocked by its darkness. It was pitch black, and she couldn't see a thing.

"Jessica," she yelled. "Are you up here? Help!"

Katie stood dazed in the dark hallway. She took a few steps, but it was useless. All of the doors were closed, and no light was entering the hallway. She heard a doorknob turn. She saw a crack of light come from a doorway. It wasn't much. It wasn't a shining beacon of hope she hoped for, but it would have to do. She ran toward the doorway. It was about halfway down the hallway. It was Jessica's bedroom.

Katie approached the door just as it fully opened. From the dim moonlight inside the room,

148

she could see two figures standing in the doorway. One was Jessica. She had a stunned look on her face.

Katie didn't recognize the other figure. He was dressed like the other two men she saw. He wore black combat boots, black pants, and a black hoodie pulled up over his head. Like the other men, he wore a mask with the eye holes cut out too large. This one was an exaggerated porcelain doll face.

The large eye holes revealed bright blue eyes, which Katie could see clearly. The mask itself was off-white, with blue eye shadow, large dark eyebrows, rosy pink cheeks, and bright red lipstick.

Doll Mask stood next to Jessica. He was several inches taller than her and held onto her arm.

"Mom," she said. "What's going on?"

Katie didn't hesitate. She knew she only had a few moments before Wax Mask would appear behind them. She decided to try something. Katie flung herself directly at Doll Mask. She tucked her head and hit him right in his stomach. She wasn't a large woman, but she hit him with all of her strength.

She felt her head push roughly into his abdomen, and he fell back and slammed into the door. It flung open and hit the wall behind it. Doll Mask when crashing just behind it. The door hit the wall and he slammed into the door a moment later. This caused the door to bounce into him and then slam into the wall a second time.

Katie felt her neck slam with pain. She must have hit him hard. In her mind, she looked graceful, like a football player trying to tackle his opponent. To Jessica, it looked like a mess of legs and arms flying into the air.

Katie pushed Jessica out of the way and into the room. Jessica stumbled backward a few steps and caught her balance. She was stunned at what was happening in front of her eyes and had no time to react.

Katie stood up and pushed past Doll Mask, who was clutching his stomach and trying to catch his breath. Katie grabbed the door that he was still leaning on and pushed her way behind it. She wedged herself between the door and the wall.

She used the wall as leveraged and pushed the door away from her. Doll Mask was still struggling to regain his balance after Katie had knocked the wind out of him. She pushed the door as far away from her as she could and lifted her leg. She placed her heel on the door and braced her arms against the wall.

She pushed as hard as she could, and the door vibrated away from her, sending Doll Mask flying out into the hallway. He crashed against the wall with a thud and dropped to the ground, his hands still clutching his stomach, struggling to breathe.

The door slammed shut.

"Lock it," Katie demanded to Jessica.

Jessica hurried over to the door and turned the small lock on the knob.

"Here," Katie said, standing up. "Help me with this."

150

Katie walked over to a bookcase on the wall, flush with the door. She began to push it toward the door, and Jessica joined her.

They pushed the bookcase in front of the door.

"Are you ok?" Katie asked.

"Yes," Jessica said. She was still shocked at what she had seen. "I think I'm fine."

"Okay," Katie said.

"What's happening?" Jessica asked. She had never seen her mother so with it and in charge.

"Some men got into the house. I don't know why or what they want. Your brother and father are still out there somewhere."

Jessica didn't know what to say.

"We've got to get out of here and call the police," Katie said. "Where's your phone?"

"It was on the bed. I don't know what happened to it. That man was in here. He may have taken it," Jessica said. She didn't notice she was out of breath.

"Shit," Katie said. "Let's see how we can get out of here."

"Maybe the window?" Jessica said.

"Let's try it," Katie said.

As they made their way to the window, Stephen faced his own challenge downstairs. Cat Mask stood facing him at the bottom of the stairs. Katie had taken off upstairs, leaving Stephen alone, in the dark, with Cat Mask.

Cat Mask seemed bolder than Wax Mask, and he charged at Stephen. Stephen braced himself for a hit. He couldn't see any weapons in

Cat Mask's hands. Cat Mask slammed into him, and they hit the ground.

Stephen landed on the bottom and smacked his head off of the marble floor. He was dizzy for a second, but his brain didn't allow that to stand in the way. He pushed against Cat Mask.

Cat Mask sat up and straddled Stephen. He took his right hand, made a fist, and raised it above his head. Stephen saw the punch coming. He lifted his arms and shielded his face. The punch landed on his forearm and sent both of his arms crashing into his face. His wrist slammed into his nose, causing him to see stars.

Cat Mask pulled back again for another punch, and Stephen braced himself again. He felt another punch land on his forearm again. This one wasn't so bad. His arm took the brunt of the hit, and his face was safe.

He needed to get Cat Mask off of him, or one of his punches would slam Stephen's head into the marble floor again. Stephen didn't realize how much he was still reeling from hitting the floor the first time, but he was sure that he wasn't going to be able to take another head slam into the marble.

Stephen struggled to get Cat Mask off of him. He tried to push back with both of his forearms into the man's stomach. That momentarily stopped another punch but didn't get him free.

Stephen had another idea. He suddenly brought his knee up as hard as he could. Since Cat Mask was straddling him, this landed

Stephen's knee right between Cat Mask's knees. The man grunted in pain. It worked.

Cat Mask instinctively grabbed for his crotch. As he did, Stephen took both arms and pushed at the man's chest. This sent Cat Mask tumbling off of Stephen. He landed on his side and briefly curled into the fetal position before trying to get back up.

Stephen stood up as quickly as he could. He wasn't sure if it was the rush of blood to his head or the hit to the marble, but he was very dizzy. He nearly tumbled over immediately, but he used the iron railing on the left staircase to balance him. He didn't look back to see where Cat Mask was as he took his first step up the stairs.

He took another step as his head cleared slightly. He relied on the railing and took another step. Before he knew it, he was halfway up the stairs. He looked back down to see where Cat Mask was. He was on his knees, trying to stand.

Stephen took another step up. Cat Mask was on his feet. Stephen took another step. Cat Mask looked around to see where Stephen was. Stephen took another step.

Cat Mask ran toward the left staircase. By the time he took his first step onto it, Stephen was already at the top. Stephen's head, while still not clear, was allowing him to move a little faster.

Stephen reached the platform at the top of the stairs and moved as quickly as he could to the hallway. When he approached it, he noticed it was pitch black. He grabbed onto the wall and used it as a guide. He knew Cat Mask would be a few steps behind him, so he had to make some progress down the hallway to his bedroom.

He took a few more steps and reached the first doorway. In his haze, he realized this was a bathroom. There was a lock on the door but there would be nowhere to hide. He continued.

He heard footsteps behind him. Cat Mask couldn't have been more than six feet behind him. He tried to pick up his pace. His head throbbed, and the darkness was even more dizzying than having some light to see.

He pressed on and got to another door. This was a closet. It was of no help. He kept going. He found another door. This was Jessica's door. He tried the knob. It was locked.

He could feel the footsteps behind him getting louder. He pressed on. He was more than halfway down the hallway now. If he could get to his bedroom, he was sure he could barricade himself inside the room and call for help.

He briefly wondered what happened to Katie. Wax Mask had chased her into this very hallway. Was she hiding in one of the rooms? Where was Wax Mask?

Before Stephen could finish his thought, the hallway in front of him was filled with light. Someone was pointing a flashlight directly at him. He froze. He put his hand in front of his face to shield it from the light, but he couldn't see who was pointing the flashlight at him.

"Hello? Katie?" He asked. There was no answer.

Stephen couldn't wait to find the answer. He quickly turned and started to move the other way down the hallway. He didn't even make it two steps before the same thing happened again.

A light shined directly at him from the other end of the hallway. This time, since there was a light also shining behind him, he could vaguely see who was holding the flashlight. It was Cat Mask.

Stephen turned the other direction to see if this new flashlight helped him see the other direction any better, either. It did. He could see that it was Wax Mask holding the flashlight. Next to Wax Mask was another man who Stephen hadn't seen before. He was wearing a doll mask.

The lights got brighter and brighter as the men approached Stephen. He frantically looked back and forth, trapped inside two haloes of light.

He looked around for a door. He found the closest one and opened it. It was a linen closet. The housekeepers kept supplies in here, and it was full of towels, mops, and cleaning supplies. It wasn't even big enough to fit a person. It was going to be no help.

He grabbed one of the mops and held it out in front of him. He swung it toward Cat Mask, then turned around and did the same thing toward Wax Mask. He was trying to keep them at a distance.

He heard a chuckle come from the direction of Cat Mask. He turned around and swung in that direction. He was closed in by both men. If they got any closer, the mop would strike one of them.

Stephen turned around again to face Wax Mask and swung again. This time, as he retracted the mop, he noticed the light behind him get brighter, and he felt the mop being yanked from his hands.

The slick wood of the handle slid easily from his hands. Stephen was helpless. He was surrounded in the hallway by the three men. He put his back to the closet door, and it slammed shut. He tumbled back slightly and rested his back on the door. He at least didn't want anyone to get him from behind.

The lights flashed in the hallway and Stephen suddenly felt someone grab at his left arm. He tried to jerk it away, but Cat Mask's grip was too tight. Cat Mask dropped his flashlight to the floor and held Stephen's left arm to the wall.

He tried to pull away, but the same thing happened to his right arm. Wax Mask dropped his flashlight and was holding Stephen's other arm. The flashlights lay on the ground, shining directly up.

Stephen had a good view of the three masks for the first time.

Doll Mask made his way directly between the two men and stood in front of Stephen. He took another step so that his mask was only a few inches from Stephen's face. Stephen struggled to get used to it.

"Now, Stephen," he heard a deep voice say from behind the mask. "There's no reason to fight us. We're here to help your family."

Stephen struggled again. He was trying to free his left arm when he felt a sharp pain in the right side of his neck. He twisted his head to the right, and the pain got worse. He noticed that Doll Mask had his hand on Stephen's neck. The

156

pain got worse, and as Doll Mask's hand retreated, Stephen caught a glimpse of a syringe. He had been injected with something.

"Just relax, Stephen." Those were the last words Stephen heard before darkness engulfed him, and he lost consciousness.

12

November 9th, 2019

Jake pulled himself out from behind the boxes. He waited until he saw no lights and heard no movement. He knew he couldn't stay hidden for long. He wanted to try to get back upstairs and help his family.

He stood up, pulled his phone back out of his pocket, and turned on the flashlight. He held it out in front of him and slowly made his way to the door leading into the screening room. He shined the light around furiously, making sure no one was hiding in the darkness.

He didn't see anyone. He slowly made his way through the screen room and to the bottom of the stairs. He quickly turned his flashlight back off and put it in his pocket. He didn't want to alert anyone upstairs that he was coming up.

As soon as he turned the flashlight off, the room turned pitch black. He wasn't able to see even a few inches in front of him. He reached out and fumbled around until he found the railing on the stairs. He grabbed it and slowly stepped up one stair. Then another. Then another. He slowly climbed the stairs one by one, holding onto the railing tightly to ensure he didn't lose his balance in the dark.

He wasn't sure if it was his eyes finally adjusting or if some light was pouring in from the top of the staircase, but he was finally able to see some shadows here and there.

The door at the top of the stairs was open. The closer that Jake got to it, the better he could see. There was some cold, blue light coming in from the kitchen.

Jake continued to climb the stairs and grew apprehensive about what he was going to find in the kitchen. Had the masked man gotten to his family? He listened but could only hear silence. That wasn't unusual. The house had a way of drowning out sound from room to room. Jake was sure it was designed that way, which was good under normal circumstances, but this circumstance just made Jake's mind wander even more.

He approached the top step and let go of the railing. He stood on the top step and peered out from the doorway into the kitchen. He couldn't see anything from this vantage point, so he took one more step into the kitchen.

He looked to his right and could see the broken glass. One of the large back windows had been smashed. There was glass all over the floor. Jake couldn't tell if there had been a struggle, but there was no sign of anyone.

He walked over and examined the glass on the floor. The way the glass had fallen made it obvious that someone had broken in, and it wasn't someone trying to get out. If they were trying to get out, the glass would be outside, Jake surmised.

That meant there was someone else in the house.

Jake walked over to the door to the dining room. He looked inside. The room was still perfectly set for dinner. Nothing had been disturbed. The candles in the middle of the table still lit the room. The food was still laid out perfectly. His mother's fine china was perfectly placed in front of each chair.

He walked back over toward the broken window. The glass crunched below his feet. He tried to step lightly, but each step crunched like he was walking on bubble wrap.

Jake made his way to the window. The window was floor-to-ceiling, and without the glass, it just looked like they had installed a glass door, and it was open. Jake stepped outside the window and onto the back patio.

It was good to be off the glass. He could be quieter that way. He looked around out back. The valleys and hills around them were aglow. He could see palm trees swaying in the breeze and vaguely hear the ocean in the background.

The pool lights were off, which was unusual, and gave the backyard a restful feeling that Jake hadn't felt in a very long time. The yard appeared empty from what Jake could see. Most of the backyard was covered in concrete and taken up by the pool or pool area. On the far end, there was a BBQ area with chairs and seating, but Jake couldn't see that far in the darkness.

Jake felt a quick vibration in his pocket. It was his phone! He had forgotten he had it. He was too preoccupied with using it earlier as a flashlight, so the thought didn't even cross his mind that he could call for help.

He pulled the phone out of his pocket and saw an e-mail notification that caused the vibration. He quickly swiped it away. He tapped away and brought up the dial pad. He dialed 911, but before he could hit send, he was hit in the head with something. It didn't hurt, but it was enough to draw his attention upward.

Jake looked up in the air at the back of the house. He immediately noticed something coming from Jessica's window. It was wide-open and Jessica was sticking out of it. She was frantically waving her arms at him. She had thrown a pen at him to get his attention, and it lay on the ground beside him.

"Hey!" He mouthed. He tried not to yell. "You've got to get out of there."

Jessica quickly retreated inside the window, and his mother popped out.

"They're up here," she said. She was yelling louder than he had.

"How many are there?" Jake asked.

"I think there's three," Katie yelled back at him. They were fully shouting now.

Jake slipped his phone back into his pocket. "I'm coming up to help you." He took a step back toward the window.

"No," Katie screamed. "They're right outside the door."

As soon as Katie said that, the door slammed loudly. She pulled her head back inside the window and looked around the room. Jessica stood right beside her, and Katie noticed the door was vibrating. There was another loud slam, and the door shook harder.

"They're trying to get in," Jessica said.

"Here," Katie said. "Help me."

She walked over to Jessica's bed and started to push. There was a bookcase in front of the door, but that wasn't going to stop them from getting into the room.

"Help me push this," Katie yelled at Jessica.

Katie came over next to her mother and started to push the bed. It was no use. The bed was a queen size with a large wooden frame. It was much too heavy for the two of them to push.

Katie ran back to the window and looked down at Jake. He was about 15 feet below them, standing in the about six-foot gap between the back of the house and the edge of the pool.

Something slammed against the door again. Katie let out a scream and hung her head back out the window. "They're pounding on the door, Jake. They're going to get in."

Jake looked around for something to help. There was some pool equipment, but nothing that was going to be useful. He had an idea.

"You have to jump," he yelled to Katie.

"We'll break our legs if we jump this far," she screamed back at him.

There was another slam at the door.

"It's not going to hold much longer, Mom," Jessica screamed.

"You can make it to the pool," Jake said. "Just use that ledge below the window."

Katie looked down. About two feet below the window was a small ledge. It was meant to be decorative trim on the house, but it was about four inches wide.

"Climb down to the ledge, then you can use it to push off of and jump out into the pool," Jake instructed.

"It's too far," Katie protested. "We can't make it out into the pool."

"Yes," Jake reassured her. "You can do it. It's not that far."

There was another pound at the door. This time, it was accompanied by the sound of wood splintering. They didn't have much more time.

"Jessica," Katie said, turning back around. "You need to go first."

"No," Jessica said. "You go first. I'll be right behind you."

"No," Katie tried to protest.

"Mom, just go!" Jessica lost her patience.

There was another slam on the door and a larger sound of wood cracking.

Katie pulled her dress up, kicked off her heels, and put one leg out the window. She used the sill to balance herself as she lifted her other leg out the window. She was nervous, and her hands were sweating. If she missed the sill, she wasn't sure she'd have the upper body strength to keep herself from falling.

She pushed herself off of the windowsill and reached her legs down below. Her bare feet swung as she felt for the ledge. Jake watched from below, holding his breath. He watched as one of Katie's feet found the ledge, then the other.

She let some of her weight off her hands and rested on the ledge which was holding her.

She heard another loud bang on the door, and it popped open. The books and ceramic items flew from the shelf and crashed to the floor.

"Mom," Jessica screamed.

The bookcase still blocked entry into the room, but with one or two more shoves on the door, the men would be able to move it enough to get in.

Katie wasn't waiting. She balanced herself the best that she could and pushed with all of her weight off of the ledge. She went flying off of the ledge, propelling herself toward the pool.

Jake watched from below as his mother pushed herself from the ledge. She got some good momentum and twisted as gravity brought her down toward the ground. Jake stepped aside to give her more room.

It worked. Katie had enough momentum that she went crashing down into the pool. She missed the concrete side of it by inches, but she made it. Jake ran toward the pool and barely avoided being splashed by the water as Katie entered the cold water.

She held her breath, but the cold water was still a shock to her system. She hadn't exactly been sober this entire time, but the pool brought her a long way closer. She felt the cold water rush from her feet to her head. She didn't quite hit the bottom of the pool and immediately began again to rise.

When she emerged, she finally clearly realized that she made it. There was no pain coming from anywhere, so she must have managed to stay in one piece. As she surfaced, she felt the air rush over her, sobering her up even further. Usually, she hated the cool night air. It reminded her too much of being back home in the freezing Midwest. But tonight, it felt comforting.

Jake leaned over the side of the pool and held his hand out. As soon as the water cleared from Katie's eyes well enough for her to see, she reached her hand out and grabbed Jake's. With one swift motion, he jerked her out of the pool.

Jake was surprised by how light his mother was. With hardly any effort, he was able to pull her from the pool. He hadn't realized how skinny she had become.

Katie regained her balance and stood next to Jake. They both looked up at the same time to see where Jessica was. They could see her face in the window.

"Come on," Katie yelled. "You can do it."

Just then, Doll Mask appeared behind Jessica in the room.

"No," Katie screamed.

They didn't have time to react as at the exact same moment, Cat Mask came sprinting out the broken window and straight toward them.

Jake pushed Katie out of the way just in time. She tumbled to the concrete of the back patio. Wax Mask tucked his head and hit Jake in the mid-section. The force of the hit sent them both tumbling back into the pool.

Jake hit the cold water first with Wax Mask coming right after him and pushing Jake down deeper into the pool. Jake struggled to break free, but Wax Mask had a grip around Jake's waist and kept him pinned toward the bottom of the pool.

After the initial force of their fall, they both began to rise back up. Jake jerked and kicked, but Wax Mask wouldn't release his grip on him. Jake flopped harder as Wax Mask pushed him further down into the water.

Katie jumped back up. She skinned both knees but didn't notice any pain. She looked around but found very little that would help her. She watched as Wax Mask pushed Jake down into the water. It was clear that the masked intruder had the upper hand in this fight.

Katie saw a flowerpot. It wasn't too big. She might be able to lift it. She ran over and grabbed it. She lifted it off of the ground with some force and felt her muscles tense in her lower back.

She let out a little grunt and carried it back toward the pool. Wax Mask was still holding Jake underwater.

Katie started to swing the flowerpot back and forth. She needed to get a little momentum going. She positioned herself right at the edge of the pool. She swung the flowerpot toward the pool, then away from it. Toward the pool, then away from it. She tried to make her move as quickly as she could.

She knew Jake was running out of air under the water. She swung the flowerpot one more time. This time, when she swung it away from the pool, it almost took her with it. She knew one more swing; she would lose her grip on it. As the pot gathered maximum momentum toward the pool, Katie released it from her grip. She took a big breath in as the pot flew through the air and straight down toward the two struggling men.

The flying flowerpot crashed directly down on the back of Wax Mask's head. He was slightly underwater at the time, so the few inches of water on top of his head helped cushion the blow. But it wasn't enough to stop it from hitting him hard.

Katie watched as the flowerpot hit Wax Mask and shattered into several pieces. The sound it made hitting the back of his head sounded to Katie like bone on bone. The pot cracked Wax Mask's head, and the water all around him began to turn a cloudy crimson color.

Wax Mask went limp very quickly, and Katie watched as Jake emerged from the crimson cloud. He came flying up with such force that he almost ejected himself from the water. He gasped for air.

"Jake," Katie screamed.

Jake pushed water from his face as he tried to figure out what was going on. Through the blurry red mess, he could see Wax Mask floating face down next to him. He looked up to see his mother motioning for him to swim toward the ladder.

He didn't even have time to think about it. He just started half-swimming, half-pushing his way toward the ladder. He could vaguely hear his mother screaming at him, but he could only focus on getting to the ladder.

He slammed his hand off of the side of the cold metal ladder. The jolt bounced up his arm and back down again. In a way, it was a welcome feeling. It meant that he had made it to the ladder.

Jake swung his arm again, this time missing the side of the ladder and grabbing firmly onto one of the rungs. He used it to pull himself up. He lifted his other arm and grabbed the rung above. He began to climb out of the pool.

He looked up and saw his mother at the top of the ladder. She had a smile on her face, and her warm look reminded Jake of his childhood. There was a warmth in his mother's eyes that he had not seen in years.

It momentarily made him feel warm inside. He missed the times he had with his mother when he was younger. They used to be very close, but over the years, his mother drifted away from all of them. She was there in body, but her mind was somewhere else.

Jake pulled himself out of the water. He was fully on the ladder. He was fully focused on his mother's face. He watched as her warm smile suddenly became cold. Her eyes fluttered and closed, and the smile quickly dropped from her face.

It took him a moment to register what was going on. Something was sticking out of his mother's neck. It was a syringe. Cat Mask was standing behind her. He had injected something into her, and she was quickly going limp.

"No," Jake screamed.

He pulled himself out of the pool just as his mother's limp body fell to the concrete. Cat Mask helped her down and stood back up to face Jake.

Jake stood on the edge of the pool. Cat Mask stood facing him, Katie's unconscious body serving as a barrier between the two men.

"Who are you?" Jake asked.

Cat Mask didn't respond.

"I saw you come in through the basement. What do you want?" Jake yelled.

Cat Mask still stood silent.

Jake heard splashing behind him. He quickly looked behind him and saw Wax Mask splashing around in the pool. He had regained consciousness. Jake knew it would be two against one. Maybe even three. His mother had said there were three, but he hadn't seen the third yet.

Jake took off running. He ran away from the house toward the BBQ area on the other side of the pool. Cat Mask took off running behind him. Jake's mind raced to quickly think of a plan. He wouldn't be able to outrun Cat Mask. The wall around the property would make it difficult to get out from the backyard. The only way in and out of the property was through the front gate.

Stephen made sure the house was set up for maximum privacy. Over the years, it had kept the paparazzi out, but now it was having the unintentional effect of keeping everyone in.

Jake's mind quickly turned to the BBQ area. Hanging near the grille were some cooking tools. Jake couldn't remember if there were any knives, but it was his best chance at getting a weapon.

Jake ran as fast as he could. He could feel Cat Mask behind him but couldn't tell how far behind him he was. Jake thought he had a decent lead, but it was impossible to tell.

The pool ended to his left, and Jake knew he was almost there. The darkness made it harder to tell. Luckily, it was a clear night, and some light was coming through the thin layer of smog that always coated California.

Jake ran under the pergola that sheltered the BBQ area. The space itself was quite large. There was a large glass table with 12 chairs around it. A built-in grille with brick surrounding it had long marble countertops on either side of it. There was also a seating area with an outdoor sofa and several chairs.

Jake wasn't sure if anyone had even been out here for years. He sprinted into the area, crashing with all of his might directly into the grille. The grille cover popped up, and Jake slammed into the knobs, pushing a few of them, igniting the grille in the process.

To regain his balance, Jake pushed himself back off of the grille. He stood up and looked at the brick wall that surrounded the grille. On the right side of the brick was a rack holding the grille utensils. Jake grabbed at the rack before he could choose one. His hand smashed into the handle of a spatula. That wouldn't do much good.

He spotted a long, two-pronged fork. He grabbed the handle and spun around. Cat Mask was standing directly behind him. Jake took the fork and lunged forward. Cat Mask jumped back to avoid the for, but he didn't move quickly enough.

Jake dug the fork into his left side, just above his kidney. From behind his mask, Cat Mask let out a grunt. Jake pulled the fork back, and it jerked out of Cat Mask's flesh. He grabbed at his side as blood started to flow from the open, jagged wound.

Jake lunged again with the fork. This time, the fork hit Cat Mask in the left shoulder. He yelped again in pain. Jake felt the fork slide in smoothly and abruptly stop and make a scraping noise. Jake had hit a bone.

He pulled the fork back out again, and Cat Mask grabbed at his shoulder. Jake lunged again with the fork, but this time, Cat Mask saw it coming and smacked Jake's hand away.

He did it so hard that the fork went flying from Jake's hand and slid across the concrete. Jake stood, weaponless, as Cat Mask lunged toward him. Jake braced for impact.

Cat Mask tumbled directly onto Jake, sending Jake flying backward. He slammed into the lit grille.

Luckily, it had only been lit for a few seconds and the grille wasn't heated up yet. But the open flames poured out from beneath the wire racks. The tops of the flames flickered and hit Jake in the back. He screamed as they scored on his shirt.

With Cat Mask directly on top of him, Jake was pinned between the man and the open flame. The flame continued to sizzle away, catching his shirt on fire.

Jake screamed again and pushed with all of his might. Cat Mask stumbled backward a little and Jake lifted himself a few inches off of the fire.

Cat Mask used all of his force to push Jack backward. Jake fell on the grille again. The fire had begun to burn through his shirt. He smelled the embers of burning cotton and the agony as the flames reached bare skin.

Jake took his right fist and brought it up with all his might. He hit Cat Mask in the side of the head. His mask twisted on his face, and his hood fell. Jake saw that he had brown hair.

Jake used this opportunity to push again. This time, he pushed against Cat Mask's shoulder. The man yelped in pain and fell away. Jake lifted himself off of the grille. He couldn't see it but could feel that his shirt was still on fire.

His back screamed out in pain. Jake dropped to the ground and began to roll around to extinguish the flame. He rolled on the hard concrete. His back throbbed as he rolled onto it, then back off of it. Pain again as he rolled back onto it, then it eased up a little as he flipped on his front.

On his third roll, Jake rolled from his back again to his front. He ran directly into Cat Mask and sent the man tumbling over him.

Cat Mask slammed into the ground, and his mask flew off his face. He landed on his left shoulder and screamed out in pain.

Jake was tangled up in the man's legs and couldn't roll again. The fire appeared to be out. Jake didn't notice more smoke, but his back was still in excruciating pain. Jake pushed at the man's legs to get them off of him. Cat Mask kicked his legs, repeatedly hitting Jake in his right kidney.

Jake yelped with every kick. His body ached all over.

Cat Mask pulled himself off of Jake and climbed up to his knees. Jake just lay on the hard concrete, moaning in pain.

Cat Mask felt around on the ground for his Mask. He couldn't tell where it had flown off to. He figured it didn't matter at this point. He climbed on top of Jake and straddled him, trapping Jake between the man and the concrete.

Jake looked up and saw the man's face for the first time. He didn't recognize him.

"Please," Jake cried out. "Just let me go."

"I can't do that," Cat Mask said.

"Why not? Who are you? What do you want?" Jake fired off questions.

"The fun of the evening is just beginning."

"What fun?" Jake cried again as the pain in his back grew. The harder Cat Mask pushed him into the ground.

"There are plenty of surprises awaiting, but we have to get everyone into place first."

"What place?"

"We just need to get back into the house," Cat Mask said to him. "We didn't think you'd be quite so…" He paused. "Reluctant to play."

"If you want money, I can get it for you," Jake pleaded.

"What is with you, rich people?" Cat Mask scoffed. "Why do you always assume everything is about money? "

174

"Isn't this about money?" Jake asked.

"No." He paused. "Well, not directly. Money corrupts. Your family should know that better than anyone."

"I have no idea what you're talking about," Jake moaned.

"I know," Cat Mask said. "I think it's about time that we go inside so you can find out what I'm talking about."

Cat Mask reached inside his pocket and pulled out a syringe. Jake saw it and began to struggle. Cat Mask easily held him down, but Jake was quickly running out of energy to fight.

Cat Mask put the cap to the syringe in his mouth and pulled it off. He spit it onto the ground next to Jake.

"Now, don't worry. This won't hurt you." He took the syringe and pushed it into the side of Jake's neck. It pushed through the delicate flesh and landed in the middle of a muscle. Jake cringed but avoided moving too much. He didn't want the needle to break off in his neck.

Cat Mask pushed the plunger on the syringe, and the clear liquid inside began to invade Jake's neck.

The liquid made Jake's neck feel flush and hot. It did dull the pain in his back, for which Jake was grateful.

"Now," Cat Mask said. "Just take a little nap. When you wake up, everything will be clear."

Jake struggled against the fog that was forming in his brain. It took away the struggle. It took away Jake's thoughts. He couldn't do anything about it taking over his limbs. He tried to keep it from taking over his mind, but the drugs were too strong.

He drifted off into unconsciousness. His final thoughts were of his mother. Had she felt the same things he had? What would be left of them when they finally woke up? Or had Cat Mask lied? And they were they never going to wake up?

Jake's eyes fluttered shut. The fog took over his brain, and his body went limp. Cat Mask waited a few moments to make sure he was out and stood up. He grabbed Jake by the left arm and started to drag him toward the house.

He looked up and saw Wax Mask had climbed out of the pool. He was doing the same for Katie. They were all going back into the Dollhouse.

13

November 9th, 2019

Katie always liked dreaming. Anything that could take her away from the harsh reality of her everyday life was part of her safety blanket. Over the years, she had developed many self-preservation tactics.

Coffee came first. It filled her with warmth, and she savored every sip. It was a habit she was never able to break over the years. When things got rough, she turned to alcohol. She drank just enough to keep the edge off and allow her to push her emotions into the deep depths of her subconscious.

That took its toll over the years. She needed to drink more and more and wanted to hide it from her family. She would never admit it, but she quickly became a functioning alcoholic. To Katie, though, the alcohol was just a tool in her tool kit she could use to keep the bad feelings away.

Eventually, they started to come back. No matter how much she drank, the feelings would push their way to the surface. She wasn't sure how to deal with them. She cried. She lashed out. She tried to translate her energy into other things. She tried parenting, but the children had grown attached to their nannies, and she couldn't break into that dynamic.

She tried doing charity work. That was somewhat fulfilling, but it felt more like a time waster to Katie than something that was going to help her long term. Katie never quite got the irony that she quit doing charity work because it wasn't helping her at all.

That's when she tried Oxy for the first time. It started as a prescription, but she quickly found that this did a great job of allowing her to function while keeping all the bad feelings away.

She did everything she could to keep it away from her family.

The thought of Katie's family started to pull her out of her dream. It was one of those dreams where nothing concrete was happening, but Katie could see vivid colors and felt warm inside. She loved the feeling, but she rarely felt it anymore when she was awake.

Suddenly, in Katie's dream, Jake's face came into focus. But that didn't fill her with the warmth the rest of the dream had. When she saw Jake, she felt panic. She saw Jessica's face. It was further away.

There had always been a distance between her and Jessica. She could feel it amplified in the dream. But, still, she had a panic feeling upon seeing Jessica. She began to breathe harder. In and out. The oxygen filled her lungs with each breath in, but none of it seemed enough.

She needed more and more and was getting less and less. She tried slower, deeper breaths, but it did not help. She tried to breathe quickly, trying to process the oxygen in her lungs as quickly as she could.

It didn't help. She began to feel like she was choking. A tightness fell on her chest. It felt like someone was pushing on her chest. Her head started pounding. It was a splitting feeling from the left side of her head.

She tried to ignore it, but that didn't work. She tried to breathe through it, but the more she focused on her breathing, the more panicked she became. The panic became a reality when one sharp breath quickly pulled Katie out of her dream, and she opened her eyes.

The room was dark. She could see movement, but her eyes wouldn't yet focus. She noticed a flicker of light and heard a voice that sounded like it was underwater. In fact, her sight looked like she was under dark, murky water.

She willed her eyes to focus. She started staring at a single spot in front of her. It was slightly brighter than everything else in the room. She could still see the light flickering in the distance, but she focused all of her attention on this one object that was only a foot or so in front of her.

She stared. The object began to become clearer. It was an off-white color. A shape came into focus. It was round. There was a darker gold edge around it. Katie finally realized what it was. It was one of her dinner plates.

She tried to lift her right hand to touch it. Her hand wouldn't move. She tried again. Her panicked feeling returned in full force. Why couldn't she move? She looked down at her hand. It was tied down to something.

A chair! Katie realized she was tied to a chair. She started to struggle and quickly realized that both hands were tied down to the chair's arms. She tried to move her legs. They, too, were bound to the chair.

Katie looked up. Her eyes were much more focused than they were before. She was sitting at her dining room table. She could see that the candles were still lit, although they had burned down when they sat down to dinner. Katie guessed she had been out for at least an hour.

Katie looked beyond the candles. At the other end of the table, she could see Stephen. He was sitting in his usual chair, his eyes open wide. To her left, in his seat, was Jake.

She had a view of his right arm. He was also tied to a chair.

Katie looked to her right. Jessica was sitting in her chair, and the rest of the family was awake. Katie began to breathe harder again when she realized who was standing between Jessica and Stephen.

She saw Cat Mask. He stood next to Wax Mask, who had dried blood on the side of his mask. He had pulled his hood down, and Katie could see his brown hair was matted with blood.

Katie kept looking around the room. Doll Mask was standing between Stephen and Jake. The details of what happened before she blacked out began to swirl in her mind. Flashes of broken glass and jumping into the pool made her anxious. She remembered how serious of a situation they were in.

Suddenly, instead of being terrified of seeing her family tied to their dining chairs, she was relieved. They were all still alive.

"Welcome back," Doll Mask said to her.

"What?" She tried to speak, but that was the only word she could get to come out.

"We've been waiting for you to join us."

"What do you want?" Katie was able to get the question out this time.

"That seems to be a popular question around here," Doll Mask said.

Doll Mask looked up at the other two masked men. They slowly made their way around the table until Cat Mask was standing behind Stephen, and Wax Mask was standing behind Jake.

Doll Mask began to walk toward Jessica, crossing behind Katie as he spoke.

"We wanted to get the entire family together for a family dinner tonight. Isn't that the family tradition?" Doll Mask asked.

The family was silent. They all stared down at the table.

"Does no one want to answer me?" Doll Mask asked calmly. He approached Jessica.

The family was still silent.

"Ok," he said. Doll Mask pulled a knife from his waistband and stood behind Jessica.

Jake grunted. "Leave her alone."

Jessica tried to look up, but she couldn't get a clear view of what was happening. Doll Mask reached down and put his arm around Jessica's neck. She tensed up. He held the knife by its handle and pointed it at her throat. His eyes went to the blade as the tip of the knife gently pushed into the flesh of her neck.

"Stop it," Stephen yelled.

"The easiest way to stop this is to answer my questions," Doll Mask said. He wanted to show he was in control of the situation.

"Yes," Katie blurted out. "That's our tradition. We were going to have a family dinner tonight for Jessica's birthday."

"See," Doll Mask said. "Was that so difficult?"

He pulled the knife away and released his grip around Jessica's neck. Jessica let out an exhale.

"We're going to have a conversation tonight and get it all out on the table," Doll Mask said.

"Get what out on the table?" Stephen seethed.

"Oh," he said. "We'll take our time and make sure everything is covered."

"Fuck you," Stephen said. "Who the hell do you think you are coming in here like this."

"Oh." Doll Mask chuckled. "I can see someone doesn't like being told what to do."

Stephen struggled at the rope that bound him to the chair. "When I get loose from here, I'll kill you." Cat Mask calmly put his hand on Stephen's shoulder to stop him from struggling. Stephen tensed up with the touch.

"This is probably going to be the most difficult for you, Stephen," Doll Mask said. "I figured you were going to be the least open to exploring…"

Doll Mask paused and looked around the room. The family was all looking directly at him.

"Your past transgressions," he finished.

This cut through Stephen harder than any knife could. He began to struggle again. Doll Mask was right. Stephen was not one to be told what to do. Stephen called the shots in his life, and even in a life-and-death situation like this, he wasn't going to give up control.

"Who the hell do you think you are?" Stephen spewed. His anger boiled over, and his face turned red. Katie watched from the other end of the table. She remembered the first time she saw him this way. It was on their first date. Their reservation couldn't be found. He got flustered. She kept him calm that day. She would do it again today.

"Stephen," she said. He focused his eyes on Katie. "Don't worry."

He stopped struggling and looked at her as she continued.

"There's nothing in either of our pasts that anyone knows about that can hurt us. It's you and I as a team. No matter what."

She always knew the right things to say to get through to him.

"Right," he said. His face began to drain of color.

"But that's where you're wrong," Doll Mask said.

"There's nothing," Katie said, trying to reassure herself as much as she was everyone else in the room.

Doll Mask stepped out from behind Jessica. He took a few steps toward Katie. When he was a few feet in front of her, he crouched down so that he was at eye level with her.

"This is a beautiful house you have here," he said to her.

"Thank you," she said hesitantly, sensing a trap.

"How long have you lived here?"

"I don't know," Katie stumbled. "Twenty years or so?"

"That sounds about right," Doll Mask said. "How did you manage to buy one of the most luxurious and sought-after houses in Beverly Hills?"

"It wasn't always like this," Katie protested. She was proud of her hours but wanted to downplay them. "It was cheap when we bought it all those years ago."

"There's probably a certain truth to that," Cat Mask said. "But it still couldn't have been that cheap back then. What? A couple of million at least."

Katie was silent.

"I bought it," Stephen chimed in from the other end of the table.

Doll Mask stood up.

"Yes," he exclaimed. "Yes, you did! You bought it with the hard-earned money from your film career."

"Yes," Stephen said proudly.

"You earned all of that money, right?" Doll Mask said to him.

"Yes," Stephen said again, louder this time.

"You're the man of the family and the provider?"

"Yes," Stephen said, annoyed this time. "Why are you asking all of these ridiculous questions?"

"Do you know why you have a career at all, Stephen?" Doll Mask asked him.

"Because I'm fucking good at what I do," Stephen was firm. He wasn't giving this man an inch.

"Well, that may be true, but that didn't answer my question."

"There's nothing else to say," Stephen said flatly.

"Maybe I should ask Katie the answer to this question."

Stephen looked down at Katie on the other end of the table. Her face had turned white. She slowly shook her head back and forth. Doll Mask crouched back down and looked Katie in the eyes.

"Katie," he said in a low, sing-song manner. She didn't turn to face him. She looked at Stephen.

"Katie, you don't have to tell him anything at all," Stephen demanded.

Katie was silent for a minute. Tears began to fill her eyes.

"There's nothing to tell," she said unconvincingly.

"I was afraid you were going to say that," Doll Mask said. He nodded at Cat Mask, who took a step closer to Stephen.

Cat Mask also pulled a knife from the waistband of his pants. This blade was longer and serrated. He walked behind Stephen.

"What are you doing?" Stephen asked.

Cat Mask took the knife and touched the tip to Stephen's hand. Stephen tried to jerk his hand away, but he was tied firmly to the chair with no hope of movement.

"Last chance, Katie," Cat Mask said.

Katie shook her head no.

"Have it your way then," Cat Mask said. He pushed down on the blade of the knife, and it sliced down into Stephen's hand. He screamed out in pain.

Cat Mask pulled the knife back, keeping pressure on it, and pulled it up Stephen's arm. The knife cut a slick path from Stephen's wrist nearly up to his elbow.

Stephen screamed again in pain. It was louder this time and more agonizing. Katie cried out. She didn't want Stephen in pain. She couldn't stop his screaming. Jessica and Jake looked on in horror.

The blood drained from Jessica's face. She looked on in horror as her father's arm turned

186

bright red from the blood gushing from the open wound.

"Mom," Jake screamed out. "Tell him. Just tell him what he wants to know. Make it stop."

Katie looked over at Jake. He was staring directly at Stephen, who was still moaning as the blood ran from his arm. Tears formed in her eyes, and she went to speak, but all that came out was a croak. She cleared her throat and tried again.

"I'll tell you," she said, although it came out in barely a whisper.

"What?" Cat Mask asked, still holding the knife in Stephen's forearm.

"I'll tell you," she said again, louder this time.

Cat Mask jerked the knife from Stephen's arm. He screamed and jerked in pain.

"Why don't you tell all of us what happened?"

14

October 8th, 1990

Katie and Stephen entered the great room at their first Beverly Hills party, looking for Gio Rossi.

Katie caught his eye and let out an over-the-top "hello."

He smiled back at Katie. He was several inches shorter than Stephen and several inches rounder in the waist. His hair, though still there, was starting to thin on top. Stephen watched as he took Katie in his arms and gave her a big embrace. Stephen's face started to turn red as Katie graciously pulled herself free.

"Thank you so much for having us, Gio. I really appreciate it."

Gio made constant eye contact with her.

Katie continued smiling and turned slightly to face Stephen.

"This is who I was telling you about." She turned her arms out in Stephen's direction. "This is Stephen."

Gio finally unlocked his eyes from Katie and extended a hand to Stephen. Stephen grabbed it and shook it with a firm up-and-down motion.

"Pleased to meet you, Stephen," Gio said.

"It's a pleasure to meet you, too."

"I hear you want to direct."

"Yes," Stephen said with a confidence that Katie hadn't heard before.

"Do you have a pitch for me?" Gio asked.

"Yes, sir," Stephen said. He wasn't sure if it was too formal to call him sir, but it was too late to take it back. "I've got a great pitch for you."

"Katie here has been saying nothing but great things about you." Gio chuckled. His gaze focused back on Katie.

"They're all true," Stephen said. "My film starts with—"

Gio cut him off.

"Wait a minute. Wait a minute. I can see you're anxious here, aren't you."

Stephen blushed a little.

"Did Marissa meet you at the door?" Gio asked.

"Yes, she did," Stephen answered.

"Great, so you've met her then. She's my assistant."

Katie chuckled. "I assumed she was your wife."

It was Gio's turn to chuckle. "My wife is probably over somewhere at the bar."

Katie and Stephen returned the laugh in nearly the exact same tone. The joke wasn't funny, but they were both trying their hardest to pretend it was.

"Look," Gio said, pointing to the other side of the room. "Marissa is right over there."

Katie and Stephen both turned their heads to see Marissa chatting with someone on the other side of the room.

"Stephen," Gio continued. "Why don't you go over there and let Marissa know that first thing Monday, you want to come into the office. I'll be happy to hear your pitch then. If it's half as good as Katie here says it is, I'm sure I'll love it."

"Yes, that would be great," Stephen said.

"Go on. Go over there and grab her now before she runs away and we lose track of her."

Gio fixed his gaze back on Katie.

Katie smiled at Stephen.

"Yes, sir. Thank you very much. I really appreciate it."

Stephen headed in the direction of Marissa, leaving Gio and Katie together.

"So, where are you from, Katie?" Gio asked. "I can tell you're not one of these typical airheaded Los Angeles girls."

"No, no." Katie blushed. "I'm from the Midwest."

"Oh, how long have you been in Los Angeles?" Gio asked.

"In some ways, it feels like five minutes, and in some ways, it feels like five years."

"Yeah." Gio chuckled. "L.A. will do that to you."

Katie smiled back at him. She glanced over at Stephen as he approached Marissa.

"Why don't we go out back by the pool? It's a beautiful day outside, and I'd love to get you a drink and learn more about you."

"Sure," Katie said. Gio turned to face the pool, and she turned in unison with him. As they walked, he placed his hand on her lower back. She was acutely aware of it there. She was hoping that he was just being friendly.

He guided her to the side of the pool, where a bar was set up. They approached the bartender, who was dressed in a tuxedo.

"What will you have?" Gio asked.

"I'll have a vodka and tonic, please," Katie said.

The bartender got to work on the drink.

"One for me, too," Gio said.

While the bartender made the drink, Katie could feel Gio looking her up and down. Katie stared straight ahead at the bartender, but it only made Gio look at her harder. He wanted her to make eye contact. He wanted to feel that connection with her. She wasn't going to give him the satisfaction.

The bartender finished making the drinks, and he handed Katie hers first.

"Thank you," she said to him.

Gio grabbed his drink off of the bar and said, "Why don't we go over here and sit down?"

Katie still wasn't looking at him so she couldn't see exactly where he gestured with his hand.

"Ok," she said, still trying to avoid eye contact. She knew she was playing a fine line here. If she offended Gio, he wouldn't keep his meeting with Stephen. Conflicted thoughts ran through her head. She wasn't sure what she should do, so she just kept pretending in her mind that nothing was wrong.

Gio led her over to the side of the pool house. There was a small seating area set up—just two chairs and a small table. This part of the yard was nearly deserted, and the side of the pool house that they were on was shielded from the rest of the party.

Gio sat down in one of the chairs, and Katie sat down as far back in the other as she could. She felt a little more comfortable because there was a small metal side table between them.

Katie took a sip of her drink and put it down on the table. Gio did the same.

"So, Stephen wants to be a director, huh?" Gio said.

Katie relaxed a little. Maybe she was overreacting before. Maybe he was trying to keep it professional.

"Yes," she said. "And I really think he has what it takes."

"Do you?" Gio said with a half-crooked smile.

"Yes. He's very talented and very driven."

"It's all about who you know in this business," Gio said flatly.

"Well, then it's a good thing we know you," Katie said, trying to sound cheery.

"I'd love to get you know you, Katie," Gio said. Katie could feel his stare return.

She averted her eyes just in time to see him lean forward in his chair and put his hand on her knee. She was glad she was wearing a long dress so that he wouldn't touch her skin.

"Oh," Katie said, not knowing how else to react.

"There's certainly one sure-fire way to make sure Stephen gets the job," Gio said, inching his hand up her leg.

She looked down at his hand and up into his eyes.

"What's that?" She asked. She didn't want to make it easy for him, even though she knew exactly what he was asking for.

"I think you know exactly what I'm looking for," he said.

"Okay," she said. His hand stopped moving up her thigh and retreated. He leaned back in his chair.

"Okay?" he said.

"Yes, but if you're going to treat this like a business deal, I'm going to treat this like a business deal."

He was amused. "And what exactly are you proposing?"

"I'm proposing that we go inside that pool house right now. I'll give you what you want, but in return, you have to give me what I want."

"What do I want?" He asked, trying to play coy.

"I've met guys like you before. I know exactly what you want."

"What makes you so sure?"

"You like to be in control," she said. "Or, I should say you like to feel in control. You make your move on someone who has less power in a situation and makes you feel high. The only way to control that high is to keep doing it and keep pushing the line further and further to see what you can get away with."

Gio just stared at her. She uncrossed her legs and crossed them again the other way, learning forward.

"Am I close?" she whispered.

Gio smiled. Katie knew she was getting to him. She uncrossed her legs and crossed them again the other way.

"So, here we are. I'm the helpless little victim, and you're the rich and powerful producer. You have something I want. I have something you want."

Gio licked his lips.

"What are we going to do about it?"

"I know what I want to do," he said.

"Then, why don't you give me a tour of your pool house?" Katie said, standing up.

He stood next to her, excited.

She followed him around the front of the pool house, and they disappeared into it.

Stephen stepped out onto the back patio at the same time. He took a big breath of fresh air and looked around the pool deck. He saw lights strung from the side of the house, fastened to poles, that looked like stars dancing in the sky.

It was just turning dusk, and Stephen could see the red sky. He stepped through the sea of people to the bar. He ordered a vodka and tonic and stood by the side of the pool, sipping it.

He looked around at all of the people. They looked so happy. Sipping drinks. Chatting with each other. He took another sip and breathed in the warm air. He wanted to be here. He wanted to be part of this crowd. He wanted to have his first shot at directing.

After the conversation with Gio, he was still on a high. Marissa promised to get him a meeting, and he was going to do everything he could to convince Gio that he was the right man for the job. He knew this was his shot; he wasn't going to blow it.

Stephen finished his drink and set it down on a table nearby. He stepped over to the bar to order another one. He turned his back to the pool house to watch the bartender pour his drink just as Gio and Katie slipped back out into the evening air.

They parted quickly, and Katie quickly noticed Stephen at the bar. She was glad that he hadn't seen her come out of the pool house. In fact, it didn't seem like anyone noticed them come out of the pool house.

Katie quickly walked over to Stephen. When she reached him, she put her arm around him and kissed him on the cheek.

"There you are," he said. "Where have you been?"

"Gio was just giving me a tour of the pool area. He introduced me to some folks."

"Meet anyone good?" Stephen asked.

"I guess we'll find out." She laughed.

The bartender slid Stephen's drink across the bar at him.

"We'll have another," Katie said to him. As the bartender turned his back to make another drink, Katie grabbed Stephen's off of the bar and downed the entire thing in one sip. "Better make it two more."

"Woah," Stephen said. "Take it easy there."

"I needed that," Katie said.

"We can't have you drunk at a fancy Beverly Hills party," Stephen said.

"Don't worry about me," she said.

"I've got a really good feeling about this, Katie."

"Me too," she said, picking up her next drink from the bar and taking another sip.

15

November 9th, 2019

Katie sobbed quietly to herself at the table. She felt mixed emotions. She never thought she would be ashamed of what she did. But she didn't want her children to find out either.

"Mom," Jake said to her quietly. "It's okay."

"No, it's not," Jessica interjected.

Katie lifted her head and looked at her daughter.

"How could you demean yourself like that?" Jessica yelled. She looked down at the table at Stephen. He sat stone-faced and looked straight ahead at Katie.

"I, "Katie stumbled. "I did it for your father."

"You fucked dad's producer," she stopped. "For his benefit?"

"Jess, come on," Jake pleaded.

"No, I'm so sorry," Katie sobbed. "I never wanted you to find out."

"That's what you're sorry about," Jessica cried out. "You're sorry that we found out?"

"No," Katie protested. "That's not what I meant."

"I'm sorry, Dad," Jessica said, turning to her father.

He continued to stare directly at Katie.

"Dad?" Jake interrupted.

"It's fine," Stephen said flatly. "I already knew."

He said it so matter-of-factly that the kids didn't know whether to believe him or not. It wasn't like their father was not passionate all the time.

"You knew?" Jessica questioned.

"Yes," he responded. Katie continued to sob in her chair.

"How could you do nothing with that information?" Jessica seethed.

"It's fine," Stephen said.

"She did it for us," Jake said. He was trying to stick up for his mother.

"So, what, Jake?" Jessica asked. "So, we could have this giant house? So, she could spend her days drunk or high and ignore us?"

"Jessica, just stop it!" Jake cried out.

The mask intruders watched quietly as the family drama unfolded. As Katie was telling everyone what happened, Doll Mask seemed almost giddy watching her break down.

"Oh, that's what it finally takes to get Mr. Cool and calm to scream?" Doll Mask asked. It brought the family back to the reality that they were trapped in.

"I'm sorry," Jake immediately said.

"We don't want anyone bad-talking your mommy, now do we?" Doll Mask asked.

"Are you happy now?" Stephen chimed in.

"Am I happy?" Doll Mask asked. "Why on earth would I be happy?"

"You got Katie to tell us what happened; now we're all at each other's throats. Isn't that what you wanted?"

"How do you know what I want?" Doll Mask asked, stepping away from Stephen toward Katie.

"I don't know what you want. You won't tell us," Stephen seethed.

"I will," Doll Mask admitted. "But we're not done with your sharing time yet."

Stephen tensed up. "What do you mean your sharing time?" He asked.

Doll Mask stepped behind Katie. He pushed her hair away from her face as she sobbed. She jerked her head away, but there was nowhere she could move it that he couldn't touch.

"We've been so focused on Katie here, but you're not innocent, are you, Stephen?" Doll Mask said.

"We've already said that we don't have any secrets from each other, so anything I can tell you will be useless anyway," Stephen said flatly.

"It's the same situation, Stephen. Katie may know some of your indiscretions, but maybe it's time the entire family found out."

Doll Mask pushed Katie's hair back again as he spoke.

"I'm not telling you anything," Stephen said.

"Haven't we learned anything from last time?" Doll Mask said, pulling the knife out of his waistband again.

"No," Jake screamed. "Don't hurt her. Dad just tells him. We don't care. Tell him what he wants to hear."

Jessica watched her brother get upset. Stephen kept his cool as Doll Mask held the knife next to Katie. She didn't seem to notice or care and continued quietly sobbing.

"Dad, just tell him," Jessica said. She had no patience with her father and even less today.

"I don't even know what he wants to know," Stephen said.

"Well," Jessica said. "He wanted to know who mom cheated with, so he seems to be implying that you did the same thing. So, just tell him. I don't think it will be a shock to anyone in this room to hear that you've done the same thing. Probably repeatedly."

Doll Mask started laughing.

"Dad?" Jake asked.

Katie finally stopped sobbing and looked up. She saw her family. Jake looked concerned, and what was left of her heart ached for him. Jessica was indignant, as usual, toward her father. Stephen, trying to maintain control, was still bleeding from his arm.

Katie finally spoke up. "Stephen," she said.

Stephen looked at her, and their eyes met. There were two decades of words built up behind their eyes. Words that they should have spoken.

Words that were easier to forget or pretend didn't exist. Words that were drowned behind vodka. Words that neither had the courage to say. Words that Katie crushed into powder and snorted. Words that Stephen projected upon everyone else.

Katie finished her thought. "Tell them about Stacey."

Jessica burst out in laughter.

"What?" Jake asked.

"My nanny?" Jessica howled.

"Yes," Stephen said reluctantly. He looked at Jessica.

"Could you be a bigger cliché?" She asked.

"Oh my god, Dad," Jake said, hanging his head back. He jerked it forward again. "You were giving it to Jess's nanny?"

"Yes," Stephen said, eyes fixed back on Katie.

Jessica kept laughing. "And that's why she left?"

"Yes," Stephen said quietly.

"Mom, how long have you known about this?" Jake asked.

"I put an end to it as soon as I found out," Katie said.

Doll Mask took his hands off of Katie and took a step back. The other two masked intruders congregated next to him. They remained quiet, and Doll Mask remained in control of the conversation.

"You're the reason she left?" Jessica yelled at Katie.

"I'm not the reason," Katie yelled. "He's the reason." She pointed at Stephen.

"Dad, how could you?" Jake looked exhausted.

"I couldn't help myself. Your mother hadn't—" He paused. "Been romantic with me in a very long time."

Katie laughed.

"Why did you have to fire her?" Jessica spewed at Katie.

"It's your father's fault," Katie insisted.

"Dad?" Jake asked.

"It wasn't me who fired her," Stephen said firmly.

"No, it was me. But if your father hadn't gotten involved with her, we wouldn't have had to."

"You can keep all of these other things to yourself, but this is where you draw the line?" Jessica asked.

"I couldn't take it happening in our home," Katie pleaded. "I had to keep you kids out of the adult matters."

"Adult matters." Jake scoffed.

"You two are beyond belief," Jessica said. "You really are. Stacey was more a mother to me than you ever were."

"Jessica, please," Katie pleaded. Tears filled her eyes.

"Oh, please. Like you didn't already know that."

"You're my daughter. I'll always love you." Tears streamed down Katie's face.

Jessica rolled her eyes. "I'm not Jake. You don't need to pretend with me."

Katie was speechless.

Doll Mask took a step out from behind Katie, and the candlelight reflected off of his mask.

"Wow," he said. The family all looked up at him. "That's great, but that's not what I was talking about."

Everyone was quiet for a moment until Jessica broke the silence. "See, there's more. It's surprising to exactly zero of us."

"Dad?" Jake asked. He was mostly stunned throughout this entire conversation. He knew his family wasn't perfect but had never allowed himself to even consider the dysfunction. Part of the way Jake was able to survive was to build up mental walls around his family. He segmented off the behaviors of his family and was able to excuse them.

His role in the family was always peacekeeper. One way he did this was by suppressing any negative thoughts he had about his family and trying to keep an optimistic outlook.

All of these allegations were shocking, and he wasn't sure what to make of them. He hadn't allowed himself to process anything about his family in so many years; he surely wasn't going to be able to find the headspace tied to a chair to process them now.

"I don't know who else he's talking about," Stephen said, trying to reassure himself as much as his family.

"Why don't you tell him?" Doll Mask said, looking over at Cat Mask.

"I'm talking about Leah Bennett," Cat Mask said.

He pulled off his mask and stepped forward into the candlelight to let the family see his face.

16

January 19th, 1994

"Leah Bennett is here to see you," a voice announced on the intercom on Stephen's phone.

Stephen was in his office, still reeling from the argument he had with Harris Goldberg the day before. He wanted Leah for the role, but Harris insisted on another meeting with the producers and casting directors.

Stephen had his assistants call Leah to his office for a pre-meeting. He wanted to make sure she was ready to answer their questions and play the part he had envisioned. He wanted them to go into that meeting as a team, ready for anything the studio might throw at them.

"Send her in," Stephen said.

Within seconds, Leah appeared in the doorway. She smiled and said, "Hello."

"Hi," Stephen said. He was standing behind his desk. He motioned for her to sit down. She crossed the room and sat down at his desk. Stephen sat in his chair across from her.

"Thank you so much for this amazing opportunity, Mr. Doll," she said.

"No, please. Call me Stephen."

"Stephen," she corrected herself.

"Well, we're not through the thick of it yet," he said to her.

She looked concerned. "What do you mean?"

"Didn't your agent tell you?" He asked.

"He just told me that I was coming here for a meeting with you and the producers, but he didn't give me any details."

"Well, that's correct, yes. But we still need to convince the producers."

"Oh," Leah said, disappointed.

"But don't worry," he reassured her. "This is my project, and I've chosen you."

She smiled at him. "Thank you so much for that."

"But we're going to go meet with them. We need to be united. You're perfect for this role, but I know they're going to have questions. I need us to be on the exact same page. Can you do that?"

"Yes," she said confidently. "Of course."

"Great, now let's talk about your character."

May 5th, 1994

"I can't believe we're a hit," Leah said.

"We are the best; there's nothing that's going to stop us," Stephen said, pulling the cork off of a bottle of champagne.

They were back in his office only 18 months later. Their film had officially opened at #1, and they were celebrating.

Stephen poured the champagne into two glasses Leah was holding. The foam bubbled over the top of the rim and ran down Leah's hand. She giggled and handed a glass to Stephen.

"To us," Leah said.

"To us," Stephen replied. They clinked their glasses together, and each took a sip from their glasses.

"I never in my wildest dreams would have imagined this would happen," Leah said after swallowing her champagne.

"It's hard to capture lighting in a bottle, but we did it," Stephen said.

He was perched, leaning on the side of his desk. Leah walked over and leaned on the desk next to him. She looked into his blue eyes.

"I think this is going to be the start of a beautiful partnership," Leah said.

"I think so, too," Stephen said, leaning in closer to her.

They met in the middle of the desk and locked eyes again. They both leaned at the same time for a kiss. It wasn't their first kiss. Stephen couldn't even remember who initiated it. They were on location for the film.

After a long day of shooting, Stephen was in his trailer. Leah came to discuss tomorrow's scenes, and before he knew it, they were on top of each other. Stephen felt a tinge of guilt. He had been faithful to Katie and had never planned to have feelings for anyone else.

They spent the last two months on location in New York together. They would dine out together. Spend their days off in their hotel rooms together, making love. The press hadn't yet started following Stephen around, and Leah was virtually unknown since this was her first lead role in a film. They were able to enjoy a level of anonymity that they wouldn't get to enjoy again in their lifetimes.

"What do we do next?" Leah asked, pulling out of the kiss.

"I guess we're just going to have to make another movie together," Stephen said. He wanted this to continue. It was a spark that had been missing in his life since Katie got pregnant with Jake.

Suddenly, pregnancy became her entire world. She was out day and night with her Beverly Hills mom friends, and Stephen felt ignored. He actually felt jealous, but it was an emotion that he couldn't bring himself to understand, let alone admit.

Leah smiled at him and kissed him again.

November 8th, 2019

"I made you. I was the one who plucked you out of that audition and made you a star," Stephen seethed into the intercom at Leah's gate.

Jake, responding to the emergency call from Leah, stood near his father.

"That was 25 years ago, Stephen. You don't own me. You can't tell me I'm going to star in your next film. I don't want to do it," Leah said.

"You don't have a fucking choice. If you don't do it, I'm going to get the lawyers on you so fast."

"Go ahead and try. You forget that I've been in this business almost as long as you. I know people too, Stephen."

"What's the problem here, Dad?" Jake asked.

"This bitch thinks she's better than me now. She's going to star in my next film. I don't know why this is so hard for her to understand." Stephen continued to pace back and forth in front of the gate.

"Leah?" Jake asked.

"He wants to shoot it in New York City. I told him no. I can't leave here for four months to do that. I have obligations here, and I'm not going to do it."

"You bitch," Stephen yelled again.

"Dad," Jake said, raising his voice. "Calm down."

"Don't you tell me to calm down." Stephen turned his rage toward his son. His face was red and flush. He had a hard time being told no. Once he was told no, his temper flared, and he had little control over it.

Before he could respond, Jake noticed a motorcycle pull up and stop a few houses down. The driver took his helmet off and was going through his backpack. Jake knew he was a paparazzi.

"Dad, look," Stephen said, gesturing his eyes down the street toward the motorcyclist.

"Let's not cause a scene here, or it's going to be online in minutes."

Stephen knew Jake was right. He took a deep breath and walked over to the intercom. He said quietly into it, "This isn't over bitch. I'll be back."

Jake rolled his eyes as Stephen hopped into his Range Rover.

"I'm sorry, Leah," he yelled in the direction of the intercom.

Leah sat inside her house, looking down at her phone, which had the intercom app pulled up on it. She watched Stephen disappear out of the frame, and Jake apologized and then left.

She sat on her couch, and a single tear ran down her cheek. She wondered how all of this could go wrong. There was no way she could go back to New York City with Stephen. It wasn't about the film or the part. She would have been grateful to have the part. She couldn't go back to New York City with Stephen because she knew what he would be expecting.

Every three or four years, he would call her and offer her a part. They'd reignite their love affair while on set, and he would ghost her again when they got back home. She was sick of it. She had sacrificed her love life and the time away from her family whenever Stephen got the idea to cast her.

She knew the worse things got at his own home, he would dream up a project and whisk Leah off to Paris or Thailand for a shoot and expect everything that came along with it.

Leah was fine with it for a while. She was genuinely fond of Stephen in the beginning, and it was 100% mutual when they decided to start things up. She even enjoyed it for the first couple of years. She was able to live her life, travel for work, and feel like Stephen's muse.

But she noticed that things started to change after she had her son. Stephen was no longer the charming man she once knew. He became increasingly possessive of Leah, to the point that he didn't even want her working with any other directors.

She was never totally certain, but she had a very strong suspicion that he had tried to sabotage her working with one of the top directors in the industry. She was on the final call back when her agent said they were going in another direction.

Luckily, Leah was never one to take no for an answer, so she boldly called up the producer to find out why. Her agent tried to stop her, but she wasn't afraid of burning the bridge. She put the producer on the spot, and suddenly, the role was hers. She wasn't sure what had changed, but she knew that there was something more going on behind the scenes that she wasn't aware of. She was sure Stephen was behind it.

She started to approach him more at arm's length, which only made him try harder to control her and her film choices. She guessed that since he had pulled her out of that audition all of those years ago, he felt some claim over her.

Leah knew how lucky she was to get that break, but she was going to be in charge of her career, her home, her family, her son, and her life. Stephen was going to have no say in that.

This film was the last straw for Stephen. She knew his intentions when he called her to tell her about his latest film, but she grew even more uncomfortable when he said he wanted to film it on location in New York City. That meant he was nostalgic for old times and wanted to get her back there.

For the first time in her life, Leah was in a position to say no. She had built a career with other directors and was getting offers. Even for someone in her late 40's, the offers were still coming. She'd done a lot of television the last few years, which really gave her some meaty characters to sink her teeth into.

She was in a relationship with a wonderful man, Derek, and they just had their three-year anniversary. She was beyond excited about him, and they'd been living together for the past year. She'd never had any problem cheating on any of her boyfriends before when Stephen came calling, but she was over it at this point.

Leah had been working hard to build an honest relationship with Derek and told him all about her past with Stephen. He was fully supportive, and she did not want to give him anything to worry about. She'd committed to herself that her days of making movies with Stephen were over. Even if he protested, which he was sure to do.

Leah just didn't figure the protest would happen in her driveway. She knew if she came outside to the gate, Stephen would just get angrier. She also didn't want to risk any paparazzi getting a photo of them arguing together, so when Stephen began calling that morning, she didn't answer. That led him directly to her front gate.

She let out a big sigh and put down her phone. Stephen was gone now, but for how long? Surely, he would be back or blowing up her phone again soon. She just had to be firm and stand her ground with him. She had more than enough willpower to do that.

Leah stood up just as she heard someone coming down the stairs. She heard movement around the corner and walked into the living room. She looked up to see her son standing in front of her.

"Are you okay, Mom?" He asked.

"Oh, yes, baby. Don't you worry about me. I know he wasn't going to be happy, but I'll deal with him. He doesn't have any control over my life."

"Are you sure? There's nothing I can do to help?" He asked.

"No, no. There's nothing to worry about, Mason."

Leah reached out and touched his arm, which was covered in tattoos.

17

November 9th, 2019

"Mason," Stephen said in shock.

Mason stood there, dressed all in black, holding the Cat Mask down near his side. The rest of the family looked up in shock. They all knew Leah's son since he was a baby. Leah had been a friend of the family for twenty-five years, and they had known Mason for all of his 21 years. Leah had even made Stephen his Godfather.

"Mason," Jake repeated in shock.

"Why are you doing this?" asked Katie.

"I'm not the one doing this," he said. "He is." He pointed at Doll Mask.

Doll Mask laughed.

"Why are you helping him?" Stephen asked.

"I don't know dad, why am I helping him?" Mason said.

"Oh, shit," Jake said.

Katie began to cry again.

"Mom, stop," Jessica said.

"It's okay, Mom," Jake reassured her. "This is literally the worst kept secret in Hollywood."

Katie took a deep breath and looked at Jake. "What?" She stumbled. "You know?"

"Yes," Jessica replied. "Everyone knows." She rolled her eyes.

"Stephen?" Katie asked.

"It wasn't me who told them," he protested.

"No one needed to tell us, Mom. We've been hearing the rumors for so long that was just had to assume they were true."

"Oh," Katie said.

"Yes, Mom. Stop crying about it. No one here is upset," Jessica said.

Katie took another deep breath and tried to pull herself together.

"There," Stephen said, turning his attention to Mason. "Are you happy? Everyone knows. You've come here to expose us, and you've done just that. The game is over now."

"This has nothing to do with me being your son." Mason laughed. "Okay, it might have a little to do with me being your son and the fucking terrible way you treat my mother. I can tell you that's exactly why he is here."

Mason pointed at Wax Mask. He stepped over from the shadows to join Mason.

"Go ahead," Mason said. "Show them who you are. It won't matter anyway."

Wax Mask pushed back his hood and lifted the mask off of his face. The family recognized his face as well, even with the caked blood that seeped from a cut on his forehead. It was Leah's fiancé.

218

"Derek?" Jake asked.

"So, he's the one that's been helping you out with this?" Stephen pushed. "All of this is revenge for Leah." Stephen looked over at Doll Mask, who had pushed himself a little further back into the shadows between Katie and Jessica.

"Is that Leah behind the Doll Mask?" Jake asked.

Doll Mask stood still and remained quiet.

Mason laughed. "No, that's not mom."

"But she put you up to this," Stephen said flatly.

"No," Derek said. "She doesn't know anything about this."

"Like hell, she doesn't," Stephen yelled.

"Would that be so bad if she did?" Mason toyed with him.

"Do you know what I could do to her?" Stephen shot back.

"Oh, I know what you think you can do with her," Mason said.

Derek chimed in. "But you have to remember now. The balance of power has shifted. We are in control of this situation now."

"Please," Katie said, mustering up the strength to speak again. "Let the kids go. They have nothing to do with this. If you want to take it out on Stephen and me, feel free, but the kids are innocent in this."

"So am I," Stephen chimed in. "I haven't done anything wrong."

Mason and Derek laughed together. "Pretty much all of this can be traced back to you,

Stephen. You're the one common denominator in this entire evening," Mason said.

"Dad," Jessica said. "You always make a mess of everything."

Stephen shot her a stare. He wasn't about to accept responsibility for anything.

"Can't you just accept responsibility, Stephen?" Katie pleaded. "Maybe if you do, they'll let us go." She was trying to reassure herself more than her children.

"Absolutely not," Stephen said firmly.

"Typical," Jessica said, rolling her eyes.

"You never accept responsibility for anything, Stephen," Katie said. "Nothing is ever your fault. You've done nothing wrong. Well, let me tell you, this isn't happening because of me. It's certainly not happening because of the children. So that only leaves one person left."

"Why don't you go and suck another shot of Oxy up your nose?" Stephen seethed.

"Oh, fuck you, Stephen. You're the reason I'm like this," Katie fired back.

"What the hell are you talking about? You have everything you could ever want. I'm certainly not the reason why you're fucking high all day, every day!"

"Now I feel like we're getting somewhere," Doll Mask said, stepping back toward the table.

"What are you talking about?" Stephen asked.

"We're finally cracking the shell of the perfect Doll family. Why, Katie?" Doll Mask asked. "Do you feel the need to suck shit up your nose all day?"

220

Katie looked away from her family.

"Mom?" Jake tried to offer a comforting voice. Jessica kept her eyes on her mother.

Katie dropped her chin to her chest and quietly said, "I need to dull the pain."

"Oh, please." Stephen scoffed. "You don't do anything. You sit around this house. You have lunch with your friends. What pain could you possibly need to dull?"

"As if you didn't know," Katie spouted.

"What is she talking about?" Jake asked Stephen.

"Yes," Doll Mask said. He seemed particularly interested in this topic. "What is Katie talking about?"

"I have no idea," Stephen insisted.

"You know exactly what I'm talking about," Katie replied.

"Dad?" Jessica asked.

"I can't keep it inside anymore, Stephen. Can't you see what it's doing to me? Can't you see how keeping this secret all these years has driven a wedge between us? It's driven me to such terrible lengths. It's turned you into a monster."

Stephen scoffed.

"Maybe this will help," Doll Mask said. He stepped closer to Katie and kneeled to face her. He pulled the knife from his waistband and held it up in front of his face. A tear streamed down Katie's face as she winched from the knife being so close to her.

Doll Mask took the knife and firmly gripped its handle. Katie closed her eyes as tightly as she could. She could hear her children shouting and protesting in the background, but it was all a blur to her.

She tried to relax. She was sure Doll Mask was going to bury the knife in her. Use it to cut open her flesh so she would bleed like Stephen. She tried to breathe. She wanted what remaining Oxy was left in her system to dull her feelings. To make her feel hazy and warm inside. But it had been hours since she had a fix. There was nothing left inside her to help.

Katie let out a big sigh and then pulled as much air into her lungs as she could. She wanted to hold it in to keep her from crying out when she was punctured with the knife. She waited for it to come. She couldn't dare open her eyes, so she didn't know where to prepare for the pain. Would it be in the chest? In the arm like Stephen? How badly would it hurt? These thoughts raced through Katie's mind.

Katie finally felt something. It was around her wrist. The ropes had been firm, and her wristed burned from wriggling. She felt the rope loosen on her left wrist. Then, quickly, on her right wrist. It wasn't the pain that she had expected. She let out the air that filled her lungs and allowed herself to open one eye to look down.

What she saw surprised her. Doll Mask hadn't cut into her with the knife. He used it to cut her arms free from the chair. She was free. Did he have something worse planned? Should she use this chance to kick him and run? Should she try to free her family? She wouldn't be able to do anything of that before one of the masked intruders caught her again.

She looked up into Doll Mask's eyes. He looked back at her.

"Take off my mask," he instructed her. He pushed back his hood to reveal slicked-back blonde hair.

"What?" Katie asked, confused.

"Take off my mask," he said, leaning in closer to her.

Katie pulled her hand from the arm of the chair. Her wrist hurt from being bound, and as she lifted it, she could feel the blood rushing back into her fingers. She wiggled them and lifted her arm tentatively toward Doll Mask's face.

Her hand met the cold plastic mask. The mask had cracks, but they were painted on, so it felt smooth against Katie's hand. She found the edge of the mask and pushed backward. The mask slid up over Doll Mask's face and fell to the floor.

Katie was able to see his face for the first time. He had dark eyebrows and deep brown eyes. His hair was dark brown and pushed back. His small yet defined nose and lips reminded her of her own.

"Who are you?" Katie asked, staring into the unfamiliar face.

"It's me," he said, looking into her eyes.

Katie began to cry.

18

February 28th, 1992

"Thank you so much for coming," Stephen said, opening the door to their new Beverly Hills home. They'd only been in it for a few months and Katie made it a point to make sure all of the decorations and furnishings were exactly how she wanted them.

She threw herself into the project to distract herself from being pregnant. She felt sick all the time and couldn't take anything for it, so she used it as fuel to build their perfect Beverly Hills home. The end result showed.

"You're welcome," the visitor said, stepping inside the house. "I'm Bonita Rokeke."

She extended her hand to Stephen, and he shook it. She was a small, unintimidating woman. Stephen guessed she was probably in her mid-50s. She had a round stature and short brown hair that she had pulled back. She wore scrubs and carried a black leather bag with her.

"Nice to meet you," Stephen said.

"Where is your wife?" Bonita asked.

"She's upstairs," Stephen said. "Right this way."

He led Bonita up the left-hand staircase. "Thank you so much for doing this. You don't know how much trouble we've had finding a midwife who would come to the house."

"No problem," she said. "Home birth is a very safe option if there are no complications."

"Great," Stephen said. "It was very important for us to have the baby here at home. The paparazzi have been following us around for months and Katie really wanted some privacy."

"I totally understand," Bonita said. They climbed the stairs, and Stephen navigated down the long hallway leading to their master bedroom.

"She's been in labor for about two hours," Stephen said. "We've called the doctor, but he's in Palm Springs. He said he would be leaving soon, but it would still be hours before he got here."

"Ok," Bonita said. "We can hope he arrives in time, but if he doesn't, I can handle this on my own."

"Oh good," Stephen said. He let out a nervous chuckle. "It's always good to have options."

Stephen led Bonita into the master bedroom. Katie lay on her back on the bed, breathing heavily and covered in sweat. She looked up and saw Bonita and smiled.

"Oh, thank God you're here," Katie said.

Bonita sprang into action. She put her bag down on the floor and walked over to Katie, grasping her hand.

226

"How far apart are your contractions?" Bonita asked.

"I don't know. Maybe a minute or two? They've been getting closer over the last few hours."

"Last few hours?" Bonita asked. "I thought you were only in labor for two hours?"

"That's what she said," Stephen chimed in. "It started two hours again."

Bonita looked over at Katie, and she looked away.

"Ok," Bonita said. "Let me examine you now. Stephen, would you mind stepping out?"

"No," Katie said. "It's fine, he can stay."

Stephen stood next to the bed, watching the examination. He crossed his arms as if he were Bonita's supervisor, ready to jump in and correct her at any moment.

Katie's breath began to get shallow, and she started to moan. "It's happening again."

The contraction began, and Katie tried to bear her way through it. She grabbed onto the sheet and Bonita's hand. Stephen stood off to the side of the bed and watched.

It seemed like an eternity to Katie, but in reality, it was over in a few minutes. After Katie was able to focus again, Bonita turned to her.

"You're almost 10 centimeters dilated. It's going to be time to push very soon. I'm not sure how long you've been in labor." She looked up at Stephen and then back at Katie. "Sometimes women can be in labor for hours before they realize it. But either way, you're entering the home stretch here. I'm going to get us set up, and I'm going to have you start to push soon."

"Stephen," Katie cried out. He looked down at her but did not respond.

"I'm going to wait this out in the study," he said, then coldly left the room.

"It's okay," Bonita said to her. "Many fathers don't want to be here for this part. We've got this."

This reassured Katie. Stephen stopped one time on his way out of the room. Katie watched as he looked over his shoulder. She thought maybe he was going to change his mind, but he quickly walked out of the room.

He traveled down the hallway and opened one of the doors on the right-hand side. He went in and sat down at a desk. Katie had turned this room into a study. There was a roll-top desk and rows of bookshelves hiding the walls. They didn't have many books, so the room was mostly bare.

Stephen sat in the chair and put his head down on the desk. He could barely hear some noise coming from his bedroom. He heard Katie yelling and the muffled sounds of Bonita shouting instructions at her.

He took a few deep breaths, and his head felt heavy. Within minutes, Stephen was fast asleep.

Thoughts swirled in his head. It wasn't quite a dream, but more semi-lucid thoughts. The first face that came into view was Katie's. She was a few years younger and he saw her as the woman he first met. She was charming, charismatic, and a great influence in his life.

Next to Katie appeared another figure. This one was darker, and at first, Stephen couldn't make out his face. Stephen didn't have a good feeling about the figure. Katie's face began to morph. It changed from full of light to how he saw her now. She was darker. The figure was casting a shadow over her.

Stephen focused on the shadow. He willed his mind to see who the figure was. The features came into focus one at a time. First, a set of dark eyebrows. Then, two deep brown eyes. A small but prominent nose. A receding hairline. Stephen recognized the figure. It was Gio.

His shadow was large and cast Katie's face in darkness. Now, she was only a figure. Stephen quickly realized that this was not a dream at all. It was his mind enacting his greatest fear.

Katie cheated on him with Gio. He found out one day by picking up the phone in the living room. Katie was on another extension talking to Gio, and Stephen silently listened. They made plans to meet when Stephen was in the office the next day.

Stephen was furious. He slammed the phone down and seethed. He wasn't sure, at first, what to do, but he wanted to confront Katie. But he had to be sure first.

The next day, he pretended to go to the office but instead followed Katie. She went to Gio's house and disappeared inside for three hours. When she finally came back out, Stephen followed her back home.

He confronted her in the driveway at home. He pulled in behind her and blocked her car in the driveway.

"How could you?" Stephen said, jumping out of his Mercedes and running over to meet Katie right outside of hers.

"How could I what?" She tried to pay dumb.

"I just followed you from Gio's. I know what you were doing in there," he yelled.

"Now, calm down," she said.

"I will not calm down. You're fucking my producer. The man who gave me my first chance. While you're four months pregnant with my baby."

Katie looked down at the ground.

"What the hell is wrong with you?" Stephen cried out.

"What do you mean what's wrong with me?" Katie said. "Why do you think you got the opportunity to direct in the first place?"

"What?" Stephen was confused.

"I'm still paying off that debt," she said.

"You fucked him so he would give me a chance?" Stephen stuttered.

"Yes," she said. "I'm the reason we have this house. I'm the reason you have a career. You would have never had the motivation to do all of this if it wasn't for me."

"Oh my God," Stephen said. He was shocked. He wasn't sure what else to say. His face went from bright red to white in seconds.

"What are you so shocked about Stephen? Do you really think that a nobody like you is just

230

plucked off of the street to direct the hottest sequel in town?"

Stephen took a step backward and looked away.

"I gave us a leg up in this business. I'm not proud of the way that I did it, but it was my choice. I sacrificed so you could get ahead."

Stephen was speechless. He thought for a moment and finally said, "But you're pregnant."

"Yes," Katie said.

"Is it my baby?" Stephen asked.

"Of course," Katie said. She stopped, looked down at the ground, then back up at Stephen. "It's your baby."

He didn't believe her. How could he trust her? It was this thought that brought Stephen back into his half-awake dream. Katie and Gio faded from his view just as a knock on the door startled him awake.

"Stephen?" Bonita opened the door and stuck her head inside.

"Yes?" Stephen said, pulling his head up off of the desk and sitting up as straight as he could.

"We're ready for you. You have a son," Bonita said, smiling.

Stephen looked at her for a moment to comprehend what she was saying. You. Have. A. Son. The words echoed in his head as he stood up and made his way to the door. Bonita pushed it open and followed her down the hallway.

She led him back to the master bedroom. She pushed open the door, and Stephen looked inside. Bonita smiled at him and stepped aside.

Stephen stepped into the room and saw Katie lying on the bed with pillows propping her up. She held the baby in her arms, wrapped in a blanket.

"Stephen," Katie said. She had been crying.

Stephen stepped over to the side of the bed and looked down at Katie. She looked up at him. Her usually perfect blonde hair was caked with sweat and stuck to the sides of her forehead. Her face was stained with tears and sweat, but her lips were dry and cracked. She softly rocked the baby in her eyes.

Stephen looked down at the baby. He couldn't get a good look at him. The blanket was in the way. Stephen leaned over and pushed the blanket away from the baby's face. He saw his face clearly for the first time.

The baby was born with a thick head of dark brown hair. Stephen felt a sinking feeling in his stomach. Stephen noticed the baby's small nose as he pushed the air out of his lungs in a huff. Stephen leaned in closer to see the baby's eyes.

"What color are his eyes?" Stephen asked.

"What?" Katie said.

Stephen looked down at the baby and saw his eyes clearly. They were dark brown. Stephen stood up straight, and eyes grew wide. He looked over at Bonita. She was standing over by the door, smiling at them.

He tried to keep his cool. "Great," he said to her. "Thank you so much for everything you've done. The doctor should be here any minute now to examine them, so you're free to go."

Bonita looked confused. She froze.

"You can go," Stephen repeated louder.

"Are – Are you sure?" she asked.

"Yes," Stephen said. "We're fine."

"Oh, okay." Bonita grabbed her bag off of the floor.

"Thank you," Katie said, with a worried look in her eyes.

Stephen hurried Bonita out of the room and watched her until she started down the stairs. He turned to Katie and stared at her.

He waited a few more minutes to ensure Bonita had left the house. He walked calmly over to Katie and stared down at her and the baby with steely eyes.

"That's not my baby."

***

The final rays of the sun peeked over the horizon. There was nothing but sand and haze covering the entire landscape. The temperature in the desert was bearable at this time. The cold, dry nights hid any signs of life. The sizzling, dehydrated days were worse. In the harsh daylight, it was easy to see that the night wasn't hiding anything. There were no signs of life. Just a dirt road and even landscape.

That made working in the desert even worse. Even though they had only been there for a few days, Ryan could never get used to the heat. He would seek shade as much as he could, but there was little to be found.

Today, he found himself standing in the setting sun in the middle of the desert. If he looked to the left, he could see the dirt road that brought him here. To his right, there was a slight hint of a mountain on the horizon. Near the mountain, he could see a power turbine spinning in the distance.

He lifted his hand to shield his eyes as the sun continued to set. The construction crew had been working in the heat of the desert all day. He moved his hand from shielding his eyes and used the back of it and his forearm to wipe a thick spray of sweat from his forehead.

Ryan squinted as some of the sweat ran down into his eyes. He blinked a few times to get it out and as his eyes began to focus again, he noticed a figure approach him. He blinked a few more times to clear the stinging sweat from his eyes. It was Jack. It was just the two of them left after the end of a long day. The rest of the crew had gone home, and they were finishing up a few things before heading home.

"I think we're about done here," Jack said as he approached.

"Thank God," Ryan said.

"You look like you could use one of these," Jack said. He put the small, dirty cooler that he was carrying down on the ground. He bent over, slid it open, and pulled out two bottles of water, dripping in perspiration.

"You read my mind," Ryan replied.

They turned in unison as Jack pointed to a large rock formation a few yards behind Ryan. They walked back to it and perched themselves on the side.

Ryan twisted off the cap on the bottle of water and lifted it to his lips. The water felt cool and refreshing on his dry, chapped lips. He drank until the bottle was half empty and stopped. It hurt momentarily. Too much cold going into someone who was overheating. He quickly got over the pain, and a refreshing feeling fell over him. He took another smaller drink as Jack began talking.

"Looks like we're the last ones here." He paused. "Again."

"Sounds about right. I hate working out here. Why can't we go back to building high-rises in the city?"

"I thought you were afraid of heights?" Jack ribbed.

"I am. But I'd rather be 10 stories up than in 115-degree heat. Besides, when we're in the city, we get started on time, and we're out of there early."

"True," Jack said. "We're always the last ones left out…" He trailed off. Before Jack could finish his thought, something caught his eye in the distance.

Ryan looked over at him to see why he stopped talking and noticed Jack staring at something off in the distance. Ryan followed his gaze to see what he was looking at. There was a car, probably a mile off in the distance, speeding down the dirt road. Ryan immediately thought that they would never have seen it from that far away if they hadn't been in the flat, horizontal desert.

The car was leaving a plume of dust in its wake. It looked almost as if a dust storm was barreling straight toward them.

"Someone's in a hurry." Ryan chuckled, taking another swig of his water.

"Right?" Jack agreed. He squinted to see better. "That's definitely a Mercedes."

Ryan squinted to get a better view as the car continued to barrel toward them. Jack was right. It was a Mercedes.

As the car bounced down the dirt road toward them, Ryan began to feel uneasy.

"Why would that fancy Mercedes be all the way out here?" He asked.

Jack shrugged. "Something doesn't seem quite right about this."

Ryan pushed himself off the rock and used his hand again to shield the light. He wanted a better look. In the distance, he could see that the car was slowing down, and the cloud of dust trailing behind it was getting smaller.

"I think they're stopping," Ryan said.

Jack stood next to him as they watched the car come to a stop about half a mile away.

The car stopped, and immediately, the trunk popped open. Ryan and Jack watched as a tall, thin man hopped out of the driver's side and ran back toward the trunk. He pulled a shovel out of the trunk and ran back near the driver's side of the car. He began to dig furiously.

"What the hell is he digging?" Jack asked.

"I don't know. This is really weird."

The digging continued until he had what Ryan guessed was a fairly large size hole. The desert sand may have been soft on top, but there was a layer of hard rock just below it, so digging a hole that size wouldn't have been easy.

The man dropped the shovel on the ground and ran over to the passenger's side door. He flung open the door and leaned inside. It wasn't quite clear to Ryan, but it looked like he was struggling with someone inside.

The man pushed and pulled inside the car. Finally, Ryan watched in horror as the man stood next to the passenger's door, pulled his fist back, and hit whoever was sitting on the passenger side. Ryan couldn't see the impact since the sun was glaring off of the windshield of the car, but he could tell the punch landed as intended. Ryan watched as the man pulled a blanket out of the side of the car. There appeared to be something in the blanket, but neither Ryan nor Jack could see what it was.

The man walked back behind the trunk of the car, out of view, and produced a box. He took the box back around the car and stood at the hole he had dug. He looked at the hole. Then, at the box. Then, back at the hole again. He was hesitating.

The man dropped the box into the hole. He looked around. Ryan could see him screaming something back to the car, but he was too far away to hear. He could only hear the silence of the desert around him.

Ryan and Jack watched again as the man filled in the hole that he had just spent so much energy digging.

"Whatever they're burying, they want to make sure no one ever finds it," Jack said.

Ryan nodded but couldn't take his eyes off the men.

Within a few minutes, they finished filling back in the hole. The man threw the shovel back in the trunk. He closed the trunk and ran back around to the driver's seat. Within seconds of getting in, the car was in motion again. It did a quick U-turn, blowing up a storm of dust.

Ryan had trouble seeing what happened next. Once the dust had settled, he only saw a brief glimpse of the car heading back out of the desert and toward town.

"What the hell was that? What do you think they just buried there?" Ryan asked.

"There's only one way to find out." Jack smirked.

"No," Ryan said hesitantly. "Who knows what it could be. We should just stay out of it. I don't want to get dragged into something that—"

Jack cut him off. "We're going."

Jack started walking toward his beat-up white pickup truck. Ryan followed him with some hesitation. He was nervous but curious about what they might find.

Jack jumped into the driver's side of the car. Ryan followed slowly and got into the passenger's side. Jack quickly started the car, threw it into gear, and drove toward the freshly filled hole in the desert.

Before Ryan could say anything, Jack pulled up beside the hole. He pushed the gear shifter into the park and hopped out of the truck.

238

Ryan joined him, and they both met at the side of the filled-in hole.

Ryan was right. It was a pretty good size. It was at least three feet by three feet. There was no telling how deep it was.

"Let's dig this up and find out what was so important," Jack exclaimed. He looked like a child on Christmas about to unwrap a present.

"I'm already sweating like crazy; it's going to be so much work to —" Jack cut him off by bumping into him. He gave him a friendly push out of the way as he made his way to the back of the pickup truck.

Jack clanked around in the bed of the truck. Ryan couldn't only partially see what he was doing, but he knew he was looking for something.

Jack reappeared from behind the truck. He had a shovel in one hand and a crowbar in the other.

"I think there's only one shovel back here. You want it, or do you want to see what you can get up with the crowbar?" He asked.

"I'll use the shovel; it's fine," Ryan said, defeated. He was in this now, so he might as well help out and dig.

Jack tossed the shovel, and Ryan caught it at the top of the handle. Jack hopped around to the other side of the hole and began to loosen and move dirt with the crowbar. Since it was fresh and loose, it was easy to move.

Ryan started to dig. As he pushed the shovel into the ground, he was surprised at how easily the earth moved. It was almost like pushing around sand at the beach.

As the hole began to get bigger and bigger, Ryan began to grow more apprehensive about what they were going to find. What if it was a buried treasure? The hole was too small to fit a body. What if it was drugs, and the cartel was going to come back and look for it? His mind raced with ideas but came to a screeching halt when his shovel hit the box.

He looked up at Jack. Jack smiled and threw the crowbar aside. He got down on his knees and began to push the sand and rocks aside. Within seconds, he had uncovered the lid of the box.

Ryan set the shovel next to him and got down on his hands and knees. The box was about the size he thought of. It wasn't completely square but was probably about 24 inches by 18 inches.

It was a hard metal box. There were scratches all over the top from where the shovel hit it and the sand and rocks had been dragged across as they were trying to uncover it.

"Open it," Jack exclaimed.

Ryan reached down and noticed for the first time that his hand was shaking. He took a deep breath, swallowed, and tried to steady his hand. He looked up again at Jack as he gripped the lid of the box.

He wrapped his fingers around the lip of the lid and pulled. It gave way and opened like a book. Ryan pushed some of the dirt out of the way so that he could get the lid fully open. When the lid was fully open, he got a clear glimpse of what was inside the box.

He unknowingly held his breath and looked up at Jack.   They were both struggling to comprehend what they were seeing. Ryan looked back down, unconsciously hoping that what he had seen the first time was a mistake. But it wasn't. There was a baby inside of the box.

The baby was wrapped in a dirty blue blanket, and everything inside the box was covered in dirt. When the fresh air hit the opening lid, the baby took a deep breath and began to cry. He was alive.

19

"My baby?" Katie asked.

"Yes," Doll Mask said, looking into her eyes. They were filled with tears, and Katie couldn't stop them from rolling down her cheeks. She raised her hands to the sides of his face.

"Mom?" Jake asked, still in shock.

Katie kept her eyes glued to Doll Mask. "This is your brother."

"What?" Jake asked.

Katie turned to face her family but kept one hand on Doll Mask's face. "Before I got pregnant with Jake, I had another baby."

The family grew silent.

Katie continued, "But the baby wasn't your fathers. So, right after he was born, your father—"

She stopped. It was difficult for her to finish the last part, "made me give him the baby, and he buried him alive in the desert."

"Dad?" Jessica said, turning her eyes to Stephen. "Is that true?"

243

Stephen looked down and didn't speak.

"Tell her that's not true," Jake said.

Stephen was silent.

"It's true," Jessica whispered.

"Dad," Jake yelled.

Katie and Doll Mask turned their attention to Stephen. He looked up to face the jury.

"Yes," he admitted. "It's true." He almost sounded remorseful.

"You tried to kill our brother?" Jake said.

"Your half-brother," Stephen corrected.

"Oh, yeah, sorry, technicality." Jake was starting to lose his cool.

"How could you do something like that?" Jessica asked.

"It wasn't my baby," Stephen said. He looked Doll Mask directly in the eyes. "I wanted nothing to do with you. I have no responsibility to you."

"Dad! How could you do that to him? How could you do that to mom?" His voice went up with each question to the point where he was yelling.

"I didn't do anything. It was her fault." Stephen paused. "For sleeping with him."

"For sleeping with who?" Jake asked.

"Fucking Gio Rossi," Stephen said.

"Gio, is your father?" Jake asked, turning to Doll Mask.

"Yes," Doll Mask replied. "I didn't find out until I turned 18 and hired a private investigator. There had always been rumors that Gio had affairs left and right around Beverly Hills. You can't deny that I don't look like him. The investigator got a hold of his DNA and tested it against mine and it was a match."

"Holy Shit," Jessica said.

"I approached him one day in the street. He tried to deny it, so I got a lawyer. He couldn't deny it anymore after the official DNA test. The only question was, who was my mother, and how did I end up abandoned? My entire record was sealed. I just remember growing up in foster care. I bounced from one house to another. I didn't have the privileged upbringing that you did."

"I'm so sorry," Jake said, his voice coming back down a few octaves.

"Why are you doing this now? You've known for years," Katie said.

"I was going to just let it go. But then came the movie."

"Oh my God," Jake said. "My film."

"Exactly," Doll Mask said. "I was happy to take Gio's money and try to forget about my past but then came that fucking movie. It's everywhere. It's on a billboard right outside my apartment. It's on my TV. It's rubbing it in my face every single day that I wasn't born into privilege. I struggled through abusive foster parents. I've gone to bed hungry since my single foster mother was just parenting for the check. I've bounced around from family to family and never felt secure in my life."

Katie continued to sob. It was very difficult for her to hear.

"Dad?" Jake turned to Stephen. "How could you and Gio let me make that movie? You knew all along. I thought it was a stupid urban legend that went around Beverly Hills."

Stephen was smiling. His blue eyes suddenly looked dark as though they were a window into his soul. "I did it for her."

"For mom?" Jessica asked.

"Yes," Stephen said. He focused his icy look on Katie. "I did it to torture you."

"What? Why?" Katie wiped a tear from her cheek and grabbed onto Doll Mask's arm.

"I hate you. I can't stand the sight of you. Knowing that you willingly opened your legs to that slimeball Gio. And I know it wasn't a one-time thing. You did it. Over and over. You didn't care who you were hurting in the process. You didn't care about anything but yourself, and for that, I've made it my mission in life to see you suffer."

"Oh my God," Katie said. "I did that for you. I did it for us. I gave us the opportunity to build this life."

"Oh, please," Stephen said. "Do you expect me to believe that?"

"It's true. I wanted nothing to do with him, but I know you needed a chance." Katie paused. "You were never going to get it yourself."

"That's it!" Stephen exclaimed. "You never believed in me or my talent. If you had, maybe things would have turned out differently."

"You're right, Stephen," Katie said, raising her voice. She tried to keep it from cracking as she stood up from her chair. Doll Mask stood tall beside her. "Where were you before you met me? You were living, aimlessly, I might add, in an

246

apartment in West Hollywood. You had no ambition, and your parents gave you everything. You needed me to push you along. If I hadn't, you'd probably be sitting on that same couch right now."

"You're lucky I'm tied to this chair right now," Stephen said.

"Or what?" Katie asked. "You're going to kill me? You killed me a long time ago, Stephen. And you used Jake and his film to beat my dead body."

Katie began to sob uncontrollably. She pushed Doll Mask out of the way and stumbled from the dining room into the kitchen.

Mason and Derek, who had been standing back to let the drama unfold, both went to follow her.

"Make sure she doesn't get too far," Doll Mask instructed them.

They both followed Katie out of the room. She stumbled through the kitchen and to the doorway that led downstairs to the basement. The light was dim, but she pushed her way down the stairs. Mason and Derek followed slowly, a few steps behind her.

Doll Mask walked over to the kitchen to see where the group was going. He watched them go downstairs toward the basement, then walked back into the dining room.

"I wonder why Mom could be going to the basement?" He asked.

Doll Mask placed his knife on the table in front of him. It was sitting just in front of Katie's place setting.

"I'm going to go check on them. Don't you folks go away. We have to finish this conversation when I get back," he said. He walked out of the room and toward the basement door.

"What the hell, Dad?" Jake said. "This is all your fault. How could you do this to us?

"You can say anything you want, but I refuse to take the blame for any of this. All of this is your mother's doing."

"No," Jessica said. "This is all your fault, Dad."

"I'm not the one who cheated," he said.

"Oh, please," Jessica said. "You cheat on Mom all the time. Why do you insist on blaming everything on her? You had a child with someone else, too."

"You used me," Jake said.

"So what?" Stephen said. "You got what you wanted out of it."

"You think this is what I wanted?" Jake asked. "I became a director because that's what you wanted."

"No, you have talent; that's why you did it. You wanted to follow in my footsteps."

"I can tell you, right now, and very firmly, that I want nothing to do with following in your footsteps," Jake seethed. "I'm my own person, and I will never allow you to tell me what to do again."

"You'll change your mind. My money and influence are too big of a draw. You won't be able to resist it," Stephen said flatly.

"I don't want a dime of your money. And, as of today, I want nothing to do with you." Jake was firm.

"Whatever," Stephen said in disbelief. "We need to get out of here. Can one of you reach that knife?"

Jake and Jessica's eyes met across the table. They both looked at the knife at the same time.

***

Katie stumbled down the last stair and stepped hard on the floor. She pushed her away along the wall. The basement was pitch black, and she couldn't see even a few feet in front of her. But she knew this floor like the back of her hand. She didn't need to see to make her way to the converted lounge.

Mason and Derek hit the floor just a few steps behind Katie. Doll Mask quickly joined them.

"Get the lights back on," Doll Mask said to Mason.

Mason pulled out a flashlight and made his way through the screening room to the storage area, which held the breaker box. Suddenly, the house sparked back to life. Light filled each room, and the hum of appliances began to fill the vast silence.

Katie struggled to adjust to the light. His eyes burned from the tears and went virtually white when the light filled the room. She pushed her way through the lounge and dropped to her knees on the cold tile floor in front of her favorite bottom drawer.

She pulled the drawer open and pulled out her mirror, a small metal straw, and her favorite bag of white powder. She pushed herself up off of the floor and leaned against the credenza. She haphazardly dumped all of the white powder out on the mirror and used the metal straw to start sucking it up her nose.

She didn't care how much she got. There was too much going on, and she couldn't face it. She needed to numb the pain. And this much pain needed a lot of help. She got two or three sucks up her nose from the straw before she felt an arm around her waist.

It was Doll Mask. He was trying to pull her away from the credenza. She tried to push him away but, in the process, dropped the mirror to the ground. It hit the cold marble floor and shattered, sending a white cloud of powder into the air. Katie pushed off of the credenza and Doll Mask let go of her waist.

Katie stepped backward and directly onto a piece of the broken glass. It pushed into her skin, and she let out a scream. She didn't even notice that she had lost her shoes somewhere. Her mind quickly rationalized losing them when she jumped into the pool, but she couldn't be sure.

She tried to take a step away from Doll Mask, but the pain in her foot made her limp. She took another step with her other foot and was able to slightly get away. Doll Mask watched as Katie limped out of the room and toward the drained pool. She was leaving footprints of blood.

He looked down and followed the footprints until he saw Katie in front of the pool.

"Stop," he said. "Just stop right there."

Katie stood near the edge of the pool and limped around to face him. She didn't notice the pain anymore or the blood pooling on the floor beneath her. She stood, putting pressure only on her good foot, and faced Doll Mask.

The thoughts in her head began to slow. She felt a relaxing haze coat her thoughts and dull the way they pierced her brain. She could still formulate a thought, but she had to concentrate harder to do it.

"Where do you think you're going?" Doll Mask asked.

"There's nowhere for me to go. I'm trapped. Trapped in this marriage. Trapped in this house. I have nothing outside of it," she confessed.

"You have your kids," Doll Mask said, half sarcastically.

"What's your name?" Katie asked. "You're also my child, and I don't even know your name."

Katie's mind began to drift. As the drugs took over, she became cloudier. It was happening faster than she had expected. She must have taken more than she was used to. She heard him say his name and the fog in her mind wrapped around it: Harrison.

***

"I'm tied down to this char," Jake said, struggling to get free. "I can't even get one arm free."

Stephen tried and was also tied firmly to the chair. "We've got to get that knife quickly before they come back. Jessica, can you get free?"

Jessica watched as her brother struggled. Now that the lights were back on, she could clearly see his blonde hair. He was sweating, and the strands in the front were glued to his forehead.

She looked over at his father. She could see the cut on his arm. The blood had gone from looking deep black in the candlelight to a bright red with the lights back on. They both were struggling to get free, but neither was having any luck.

Jessica's mind turned to her mother and the intruders. What was happening to them in the basement? Jessica turned to her father.

"Yes," she said. "I can get free."

Jessica stood up. There were no ropes on her. The arms of her chair were below the table, so no one could tell she wasn't bound to the chair like the others.

"What the hell?" Stephen said.

"Where are the ropes? Jake asked.

Jessica walked over and grabbed the knife off of the table. "I was never tied down." She looked at Stephen. "I'm the one who is behind this all."

20

November 8th, 2019

Jessica sat in the apartment with Mason and Harrison, waiting for Mason to roll a joint.

"Won't your parents wonder why you came home from school stoned?" Harrison asked.

"I don't think my parents would even notice if I didn't come home from school most days," Jessica responded. She still didn't look at him.

"Sorry, you're the poor little rich girl, right?" Harrison snapped.

"Look, I don't have to stay here right now. I can walk right out the door," Jessica responded with anger.

"Woah, woah, woah," Mason said, trying to smooth the tension. "It's fine. We're going to light this thing up, and everything is going to be ok."

Jessica wasn't sure if anything was going to ease the tension in the room. Mason finished rolling the joint and handed it to her. She grabbed the lighter from off the table and lit up the joint. She inhaled deeply and took all of the smoke into her lungs. She held her breath as long as he could and calmly exhaled the smoke.

She felt a quick calming effect. She passed the joint to Harrison, who did the same. He passed it back to Mason.

Before Mason took a long puff, he said, "See, now, doesn't that feel better?"

Jessica was starting to relax. She looked Harrison in the eyes for the first time and could tell he was relaxing, too.

She took another deep breath and let go of her anxiety.

"What time is he getting here?" Jessica asked.

"He should be here any minute," Mason replied.

Harrison continued to stare at Jessica. She took another deep puff of the joint, then reached over to pass it to him. He took it from her and took a puff.

"This is really weird," she said. Harrison continued to stare at her but didn't speak. "So, you're my brother?"

"Yes," he said, stone-faced.

"How long have you known?"

"A while now," Harrison said.

"The private investigator is going to tell us what happened?" She asked.

"I know what happened," he said. "Your father is an asshole."

"I'm not going to disagree with that." Jessica chuckled.

There was a knock at the door. Mason disappeared from the room to open the door. Jessica could hear him greeting someone from the other room. The uncomfortable space between her and Harrison was interrupted when Mason returned to the room with the private investigator.

Jessica looked up at him. She immediately recognized him. It was Derek.

"You're the investigator?" She asked.

"It's me," he said, sitting down on the bed next to her. "Are you sure you want to know all of this?"

Jessica took a deep breath. "Yes, I need to know."

"Okay," he said. "Here's what I found out." He handed her a large manilla envelope.

"Do you want me to tell you what's in there? Or do you want to read it yourself?"

"You can tell me," she responded.

Derek looked around the room. Harrison and Mason were all focused on Jessica. They wanted to see how she would react to the news.

"Well," Derek began. "It started back in the early 90's. Your mother had an affair with your father's producer, Gio Rossi. I'm not sure how or why exactly, but it may have been some sort of 'me too' type of situation.

"She had an affair that went on for months. Eventually, she found out she was pregnant. Your father found out about the affair and was furious. I can't find any record of a DNA test, so I don't know if they ever knew for sure, but your father thought the baby was Gio's. He wanted nothing to do with the baby. In fact, it's much worse than that. He actually actively tried to kill the baby.

"Shortly after the baby was born, he drove your mother to the desert, ripped the baby from her arms, and buried him alive in the desert. Luckily, two construction workers witnessed the entire thing and saved the baby."

"Shit." Jessica hung her head.

"That's me," Harrison chimed in.

"How did they not know the baby survived?"

"Good Question," Derek continued. "The police were very interested in who did this. So, they kept the press from it while they investigated. Harrison went into the foster system, and the police were never able to come up with any leads. They only thing they knew for sure was that it was a Mercedes that dropped off the baby.

"Somehow, that information leaked out, and it became the talk of the town for a little while in Beverly Hills. Since there was never any proof, it spread like a game of telephone and morphed along the way.

"I can only assume your mother heard it and had a breakdown. That couldn't have been easy on her. Unless, of course, she was in on it. But I don't think that was the case.

"Your father then proceeded to sleep with everyone in town. It was no secret that he had a casting couch in his office. Leah was among the women that he bedded. She claims to this day it was consensual, but I'm not totally convinced. That leads us to Mason."

"Yes," Jessica said. "He's also my brother."

"Yes," Derek replied. "That gossip has gotten around town many times, so I'm sure your mother is aware of that, too."

"How can they mess with so many lives like that?" Jessica said. Her face began to get red with anger, just like her father's.

"I told you that your father was an asshole," Harrison said.

"We've got to make them pay," Jessica said.

"I don't think your mother had anything to do with it," Derek repeated.

"Yes, she does. She knows about all of this. She has been complacent and allows him to get away with it. She's in a position to take him down and never has."

"I honestly don't think your mother has the frame of mind needed to take down someone like your father," Derek said.

"Good thing I do," Jessica said.

***

Jessica fumed the entire way home. Everything that Derek told her rattled around inside her brain. She wasn't sure how to process everything at once, so she tried to take it one step at a time.

By the time she got to the house, she was so angry she immediately went looking for her mother. She wasn't sure what she was going to say, but she needed to see her.

As usual, she found Katie in the lounge in the basement. She was semi-conscious on the couch.

"Mom," Jessica shouted to alert her presence.

Katie half opened her eyes, "Jessica?"

Derek's words continued to bounce around in her head. Her father tried to kill her brother. Her father had an affair and a child with Leah. But that just made Jessica wonder why she and her mother weren't closer. Surely, after all of that so early in her marriage, wouldn't that make her closer to her children?

Jessica had to know, "Mom?" she asked again. Katie stirred but didn't respond. "Why aren't we closer?"

"What are you talking about?" Katie slurred.

"You and Jake are close. You two always had a connection. You always seem to…" Jessica trailed off as she struggled for words. "Keep me at arm's length."

Katie tried to pick her head up off of the back of the couch. It was no use; she didn't have enough strength. Instead, she just rocked her head back and forth, left to right.

"Come on, Mom," Jessica said. "I thought maybe you'd want to just be honest with me for once in your life when you're like this."

"You want me to be honest?" Katie said. She opened her eyes halfway.

"Yes," Jessica said.

Katie grabbed Jessica's arm and pulled herself up the best that she could. She struggled to maintain her balance, even sitting to remain upright. "This isn't something you're going to want to hear."

"Yes, it is," Jessica insisted.

Katie closed her eyes and slightly opened them again. "About nine months before you were born, your father came home drunk one night."

"Surprising," Jessica said, rolling her eyes.

"He'd been at his office with God-knows-who, and they were drinking. He smelled of liquor, and he could barely stand. I'm not quite sure how he even managed to drive home."

Katie paused. She got lost in her thoughts. Jessica touched her arm, and it brought her back.

"When he got home, I was already asleep in bed. By this point, I knew he had been sleeping with Leah and probably every extra on one of his sets. But that was okay with me at the time."

"Why would that ever be okay?" Jessica asked.

"Because it kept him away from me. I didn't want anything to do with him like that anymore."

Jessica understood.

"But, that night, it didn't keep him away from me."

Jessica took a deep breath.

Katie continued, "he stumbled his way into the bedroom and fell onto the bed. I tried to get up, but he was lying to me. He started to grab me, and I tried to push him off. I told him no, but I don't even know if he could hear me or comprehend me."

"Mom," Jessica said sympathetically. She tried to look into her mother's eyes, but they were rolling into the back of her head as she swayed and talked.

"I tried to tell him no," Katie said again, starting to drift off.

"It's okay, Mom," Jessica said. "You don't have to tell me anymore."

Katie fell back onto the couch into a state of semi-unconsciousness. Jessica made sure she had a pillow under her head.

This was the first time she felt like her mother was ever honest with her. Now she knew why, and she wanted her father to pay. She was finally able to connect with her mother. A moment was better than none at all.

21

November 9th, 2019

"You've gotten away with this for far too long," Jessica said to Stephen. She stood over him, clutching the knife in her hand.

"Jessica, don't do this," Jake screamed at her.

Jessica walked over to Jake. "Do you know why I'm here?"

"What?" Jake asked, confused by the question.

"Do you know why I exist?"

Jake looked up at her and saw pain in his sister's eyes. It had always been hidden before, but it was front and center right now. He'd never taken the time to really think about why there was a dark cloud always over Jessica's head. He just thought it was growing pains. Typical teenage stuff. He'd been through it, too, but Jessica just let it get to her.

Jessica was younger than him. He'd always seen himself as her protector. He'd never taken the time to get to know what she thought she needed to be protected from. He knew that his mother never afforded Jessica the same comforts that he had. He had always been the favorite; there was no denying that, but he never felt that drive a wedge between him and his sister. He did know that drove a wedge between Jessica and their mother, though.

"Why?" Jake asked. "What are you getting at?"

"Mom finally told me. I guess the drugs are good for something. The only reason that I'm here is that he raped her."

Jessica pointed at Stephen.

He laughed. "What are you talking about? You can't rape your wife."

"That's your defense?" Jessica laughed.

"Dad, what is she talking about?" He felt like a broken record at this point. He was behind everyone else in the family.

"He came home drunk one night. Mom said no. He didn't listen. What would you call that?" Jessica scoffed.

"Why would your mother say no to me?" Stephen asked. Jessica wasn't sure if that was a serious question, but she was fully prepared to answer it.

"Because you're a narcissist. You're the classic textbook definition. Mom was guilty of feeding your ego. Hell, she was probably the one in charge of building it. But you turned into a monster. You stuck your dick in places it didn't belong, and when mom didn't want you anymore because of it, you just took whatever you wanted."

"Oh, please. Your mother knows exactly what she's doing. She knows when she fucks someone and claims it's for my career. She knows when she has another man's baby. She knows when she snorts that shit up her nose. She's in complete control of her actions," Stephen yelled.

"And you're in control of yours," Jessica said.

Jessica looked over at Jake. She saw her big brother's eyes. They looked confused but still comforting at the same time. She leaned over him and used the knife to sever the ties that held him to the chair, one arm at a time.

"Thank you," Jake said, rubbing his wrists, trying to get the blood to circulate and return feeling to his hands. Now, untie Dad so that we can end this."

Jessica turned to Jake. She was standing right next to him, looking him in the eye. He was a few inches taller than her. She reached down and pulled something out of her pocket. It was the Tech Deck mini skateboard that Jake had given her years ago.

"Do you remember this?" Jessica asked.

"Of course, I remember that," Jake said. "That was my lucky Tech Deck that I gave to you. You still have it."

"Yes, I totally do," Jessica said. "I carry it around with me everywhere I go."

She grabbed Jake's hand and held it. Jake squeezed back.

"Do you remember the conversation we had that day?" She asked.

"Yes," Jake responded. "Like it was yesterday."

"You told me you were always going to be there for me. Even if I couldn't rely on Mom and Dad, you were my big brother, and you were going to be a rock for me."

"Yes, that's what I said."

"I need you to help me today," Jessica said.

Jake let out a little laugh and pulled his hand away from hers. "I didn't mean that I would help you attack Mom and Dad."

"I'm sorry that you and Mom got caught up in this. This is really about Dad. Although Mom's not innocent, Dad was the one who dragged her into all of this."

Stephen let out a large laugh. It almost sounded like a supervillain's evil cackle.

"See," Jessica said. "Nothing we can say or do is ever going to make him take any responsibility for his actions. He thinks he's right all the time. We've tried. Nothing will work."

Jake looked over at Stephen, who had a shit-eating grin on his face. Jessica was right.

"But…" Jake thought for a moment. "Don't you remember the conversation you had with Leah earlier that day? I know you two have gotten close over the years."

"I remember that too," Jessica said.

"Leah told you to choose love. I know you took that to heart. This isn't choosing love."

"But it is," Jessica said. "I've tried. So many times over the years to get Dad to admit that he's an asshole. But he won't. I've tried to get closer to Mom, but the barrier won't let us. The drugs haven't helped the situation either."

"But," Jake tried to interrupt.

"Let me finish," Jessica said. "I need to get the poison out of our lives. I'm doing this for me and you. We can't truly choose love when the person at the head of our family continues to choose lies and hate. Our eyes have now been opened to all of the terrible things he's kept hidden all of these years. Love can't overcome it until we cut out the hate and discard it."

"I guess that makes sense," Jake said, more confused than ever.

"You're not buying this load of shit, Jake. Come on. You're just like me. You're better than this," Stephen seethed.

"I'm nothing like you," Jake replied, looking at his father. "I'm absolutely nothing like you. I've always chosen to keep the peace. I've tried to keep your hurtful comments away from Mom. Tried to make sure I was there for Jess when you couldn't give a damn."

"Oh, please. You're making yourself out to be some kind of saint," Stephen said.

"I am." Jake took a breath. "Compared to you."

Jake looked back over at Jessica. She was still holding the Tech Deck in her hand. She slid it open to show him inside. It was empty. Jake knew where the key was.

"You gave them the key. That's how they got inside unnoticed."

"Yes," Jessica said. "I didn't realize it, but all those years ago, you gave me the key. The key was the answer to our problems."

Jake grabbed her hand again and squeezed. Jessica used her free hand to pull her phone out of her pocket. She entered her passcode and tossed it on the table in front of Jake.

"Check on mom downstairs?" Jessica asked.

Jake looked at her and squeezed her hand. He made his decision. He was with Jessica. He grabbed the phone, brought up the camera app, and tapped on the camera in the lounge in the basement. He didn't see anyone. He flipped through the cameras until he found his mother standing near the edge of the drained pool. Harrison was standing a few feet in front of her.

"Shit," Jake exclaimed. "They have her cornered." He turned around as quickly as he could. He'd been immobile for so long that the blood immediately rushed to his head, and he stood dizzy for a moment. He took a deep breath and made his way as quickly as he could out of the dining room and toward the basement.

Jessica turned her attention back to Stephen. "That's it, Dad, right?"

"You've been driving this conversation, you tell me."

"Yes." Jessica chuckled. "That's it. At least, I think that's it. So that means there's nothing left to talk about."

"Great," Stephen said. "You can untie me now."

Jessica stepped over to him. She stood over him with the knife clutched in her right hand.

"Were you listening to any of that?" Jessica asked.

"What? I heard it," Stephen said. "You want me to take the blame for everything that's wrong with this family. Your mother should be up here if you want someone to blame."

Stephen looked up at her with his piercing blue eyes. He looked past the pain in Jessica's eyes. He never really saw her, and this time was no different. He looked down at the ground and back up again into her eyes.

"This is for Leah. This is for Mason. This is for Harrison. This is for Jake. This is for Mom. And most of all, this is for me."

Jessica plunged the knife deep into Stephen's chest. He was never going to change. He was never going to admit that anything he had done was wrong.

Stephen looked shocked. He stared down at the knife as rich, warm red blood began to flow out of his chest and warm the entire front of his body. He felt the pain of the knife, but not in a way that could be described. His body was in shock and was protecting him from feeling the deep pain as the knife lodged itself in his heart.

It quickly became hard for him to breathe. He tried to pull oxygen into his lungs, but they wouldn't receive it. That caused a panic inside him. His eyes suddenly grew wide, and he looked at Jessica again. She was standing over him with a smirk on his face.

He tried to speak, but no words would come out. It became even harder to breathe, and he noticed that the room behind Jessica was beginning to face.

The darkness came quickly as the walls faded. The candle lights that once illuminated the room were now dull flickers behind Jessica. Soon, Stephen could only focus on his daughter's face.

He stared at her again as she looked back at him, satisfied. He tried again to formulate words. He wanted to ask for help. He wanted her to stop him from fading.

As Jessica's face slowly began to fade into the overwhelming darkness, the words I'm sorry never crossed Stephen's mind. His final thought was a question. What would happen to his office at the studio?

***

Jake pushed his way quickly down the stairs. He turned toward the empty pool at the bottom and found Katie. It was just like he saw on the camera. She was standing, bleeding from one foot, near the side of the pool. Harrison stood a few feet away from her, with Mason and Derek slightly further back.

"Mom," he yelled, running toward her. Harrison grabbed him to stop him from getting too close, and the two men stood side by side.

Jake watched as Katie stood, swaying from side to side. Her eyes were partially open, and she stood balancing on one foot to keep from putting pressure on her injury.

"Jakey, baby," Katie said to no one in particular.

"Mom, I'm here."

Harrison watched as Jake talked to his mother.

"What did you do to her?" Jake asked Harrison.

"Nothing," Harrison said. "She made a run for the drugs and sucked who knows how much up her nose before we stopped her."

"She's bleeding," Jake said.

"She broke the mirror and then stepped on it. This was all her own doing."

Jake turned back to Katie. "Mom? Come over here; I'll help you."

Katie didn't respond. She stood there, swaying. Jake had seen her look like this plenty of times. She was somewhere else. Somewhere, she felt more comfortable.

Jake had always wondered why she never felt comfortable with her children or in this house. He had a general understanding of why she never felt comfortable with Stephen. Jake had never seen much of a spark or any love between the two his entire life. But that was just the reality of growing up in Beverly Hills.

He saw it with so many of his friends, too — rich people letting money corrupt them. He never knew the pain that ran so deep in his family. He briefly wondered if they all had secrets like these.

"Jake, I'm sorry," Katie muttered.

"Let me get her," Jake said, trying to reason with Harrison.

"We have to wait," Harrison replied.

"For what? She's obviously injured and high. At least let me get the glass out of her foot and wrap it up."

"Jessica will be down in a minute," Harrison said.

"I'm here," a voice said from behind them. Jessica emerged from the doorway and joined Harrison and Jake. Katie's three children were lined up in front of her.

"Hey," Harrison screamed, trying to bring Katie back to reality.

Katie opened her eyes and looked at them. She saw Jake first. She always saw Jake first. Jake would always be a child to her. She wanted nothing more than to be able to go back and be the mother Jake deserved. The mother who would take him to the park and attend all of his school plays. She wanted to support him throughout his career. She wanted to be the shoulder he could lean on. But she wasn't strong enough.

She wasn't strong enough to put the past behind her. She wasn't strong enough to lock all of the shattered moments in her life away in her brain. They gnawed and pecked at her every chance they got, and getting high was the only way that she could get away from them.

Katie saw Jessica. She looked at her differently now. She knew the truth. She knew why she couldn't connect with her and love her the way she loved Jake. Katie tried so hard over the years, but she wasn't strong enough to get past what Stephen had done and how Jessica came into the world.

Katie saw Harrison last. She had thought about him every day for the last twenty-something years. This wasn't the way that he was supposed to come into the world, and this surely wasn't the way they were supposed to meet. She felt the emotions welling up inside of her. As usual, they were too overwhelming for her to even think about, so she willed the drugs to take over again. She wanted them to numb the pain and take away the emotions she tried so hard to forget.

This time was different, though. It wasn't working the same. Maybe she had taken too little. Or maybe she had taken too much. She wasn't sure, but she stood there, eyes open again, facing her children.

"Harrison," she said. "I never stop thinking about you. I never stop thinking about that day. I should have been stronger and not let Stephen do that to you. It eats at me from the inside and has left me nothing but a shell of a human.

"Jake. You're my baby boy. You always will be. I'm so proud of you. You saved me in more ways than you know.

"Jessica. I'm so sorry that life has dealt you the shitty hand that it has. You deserve better than me. You deserve better than this place."

Katie felt the emotions inside her begin to overtake her brain. She never felt it like this before. It was a wave that warmed her entire body and made her mind into jelly. She couldn't formulate a thought. She couldn't speak. She could only feel everything that she had been pushing down for so long.

She cried inside for Harrison. She cried for not fighting for him and allowing Stephen to bury him in the desert like that. She wept for Jake and the life he deserved. She lamented for not being a better mother to Jessica and giving her the same privileges and love in life that Jake enjoyed.

Katie cried for herself. She regretted ever letting Gio take advantage of her like that. She regretted not telling him no the first time. She used her body to build this life, and now the only thing she had left was a hollow shell with no soul inside.

She was sorry she allowed Stephen to push her around for so long. She regretted being his perfect Beverly Hills wife. It was all a lie. The Dolls were not perfect. No one was perfect. Certainly not Katie. She didn't want to live a lie anymore. It had cost her too much. It cost her one of her children. It cost her the love of another one of her children.

Katie managed to look down and focus her eyes. She realized that she was standing at the edge of the drained pool. She looked down at the cold, decaying marble, and tears began to fill her eyes. She remembered buying the house with the pool and the promise that it held. All of that promise drained from her body little by little, leaving her to feel like a shell of a person.

The wave began to overtake Katie. This time, the drugs were working. The emotions went away quickly, and Katie went limp. She tried to catch herself, but the pain coming from the glass in her foot was too much.

"No," Jake screamed when he realized what was happening. He pushed Harrison to the side and ran toward Katie. But he wasn't close enough.

Katie's limp body fell backward over the side of the drained pool. Jake lunged toward her but only brushed the side of her dress as she fell backward.

It was eight long feet down to the porcelain tile of the pool. A fantasy played out in Katie's head as she fell. The family was happy. She and Stephen sat around the dinner table with their three children, smiling and laughing. It brought a smile to Katie's face.

She wanted nothing more in life than her family. Her fantasy was shattered when Katie hit the bottom of the pool. Her head hit the cold porcelain tile, cracking it open.

Katie didn't feel anything. She was too busy thinking of her perfect family as her mind went dark, and she drifted off into the darkness.

The blood drained from the back of her head, gathering around her exhausted body as her children stood at the pool's edge, looking down at her. Jake was still screaming. Harrison stood shocked. A tear rolled down Jessica's cheek for the mother who never loved her.

EPILOGUE

The next afternoon found them gathered in Leah's airy dining room — still too soon after the tragedy, yet somehow exactly where they needed to be. A few cardboard takeout boxes sat at the center of the table, the plastic lids half-open, releasing the faint aroma of pad thai and dumplings. It wasn't elegant or home-cooked, but it was the best Leah could manage. She was trying, though the hesitation in her eyes spoke volumes.

"Sorry," she said, smoothing a hand over the edge of the table. "I'm no chef, so takeout seemed like the safest option." Despite her casual tone, her gaze flicked over each face, like she was testing out a new role — part host, part matriarch, still uncertain if it fit.

Across from her, Jessica carefully opened a container of noodles, setting them down between herself and Mason. A half-step away, Harrison hovered, arms folded, looking around with subdued tension. He'd let out a small sigh of relief when he first walked in as if allowing himself — just for a moment — to feel he might belong.

Jake offered a quiet thanks to Leah, then took a seat. "At least you saved us from one of those fake fancy dinners," he murmured. A flicker of something close to amusement passed between them, though neither quite smiled.

They were all battered — physically or otherwise — but unburdened of secrets. No one needed to pretend at perfection anymore.

Leah reached for a set of paper plates, distributing them around. Her voice came out calm, but the slight quiver in her hands gave her away. "We'll figure this out. Together."

They picked at the meal quietly, with no forced etiquette, just silent, cautious acceptance. Eventually, Jessica cleared her throat. "I — I wanted to say thank you. For letting us be here, Leah." Her words felt heavy in the hush. "I know none of this is what we expected."

Leah nodded, gaze steady if uncertain. "I just…couldn't imagine us anywhere else." She swept a glance toward Harrison, who stood a bit removed from the table. Slowly, he eased onto the chair beside Mason, exhaling as if trying to settle. He still looked guarded, but he was here — that counted for something.

A spasm of emotion crossed Mason's face. He caught Jessica's eye and grinned a tiny, honest gesture. A moment shared: as if they'd been siblings all their lives and not just two kids bound by a twisted secret.

Jake cleared his throat. "Well, about next steps...I spoke to the realtor. The house sold. Finally."

A flicker of relief, or perhaps resignation, crossed everyone's features — one less piece of the old life to cling to.

Leah nudged an unopened box of dumplings closer to Harrison. "We'll...figure out logistics," she repeated softly, voice wavering. "But for today, just eat. Rest."

Jessica's eyes dropped to her lap. For the briefest moment, she almost smiled — almost. This was the closest she'd come to a family meal that didn't feel forced. The sense of calm was tentative, but it was real. Even Harrison's shoulders relaxed, just slightly, as if he might allow himself to trust this new, fragile bond.

Then, from somewhere beyond the open window came a faint siren. It echoed in the distance, drawing nearer with each passing second. Everyone went still as the wail threaded through the quiet room. Leah and Jake exchanged a look of dread while Mason's jaw set tight. Harrison's gaze darted to Jessica, uneasy.

Jessica rose slowly, setting her disposable fork aside. She caught the worried expressions on their faces. "Don't," she whispered as if they might try to stop what was inevitable. "We knew they'd come."

No one else spoke. The hush felt heavier than before. Jessica's eyes swept around the table — over Leah, who'd tried so hard to hold it together, over Harrison and Mason, both newly bound to her in a truth none of them had asked for. Finally, she looked at Jake, her constant since childhood.

She managed a gentle press of her hand to his shoulder. "I'm…glad I had this," Jessica said quietly, her voice trembling just enough to betray how much it mattered. "Even if it's just for one day."

Outside, a car door slammed. The siren abruptly cut off, leaving only an ominous silence in its wake. Jessica let herself have one last look at them—this strange, patchwork family table, no secrets, no forced smiles. A perfect moment in a life that had known too few.

Then she exhaled, stepping away. In that fleeting breath, they could all see her accepting the sacrifice. She had done what needed to be done—she had created this delicate peace, even though it wouldn't last.

Jake's voice wavered as he said her name, but Jessica merely shook her head, a quiet command for him not to follow. The day's warmth fell away, replaced by the chill knowledge of what awaited beyond that door.

Yet, for one final heartbeat, she stood in the glow of this honest gathering, tasting the single moment of togetherness she had yearned for. The siren might have stopped, but everyone knew what it meant. Her time in this fragile sanctuary was over.

Jessica turned, slipping into the hall. Behind her, the others remained, unified in the stillness. Whether they would see her again after this was anyone's guess.

She carried with her the memory of that short-lived freedom—no secrets, no masks, just a family. And the sound of distant steps outside, creeping closer, was all the proof she needed that she would do it again in a heartbeat.